FINALLY MATCHED

CATHRYN BROWN

For permission requests, write to the publisher, addressed "Attention:
Permissions Coordinator," at the address below.

Sienna Bay Press

PO Box 158582

Nashville, Tennessee 37215

www.cathrynbrown.com

Cover designed by Najla Qamber Designs

(www.najlaqamberdesigns.com)

ISBN: 978-1-945527-35-7

Finally Matched/Cathryn Brown. - 1st ed.

❀ Created with Vellum

DEAR READER

Mark and Madeline, Maddie as Mark calls her, met when they were babies. On their first day of high school, he saw her across the room and something changed in him. He finally got up the nerve to ask her out and they were inseparable from that day forward. Until they were eighteen and she broke up with him.

They haven't talked to each other in the fifteen years since then. Until . . . a matchmaker brings them together. It's a charming second chance romance.

And if you love HGTV like I love HGTV, then you'll enjoy Madeline's house construction and design. I had fun writing those sections of their story.

The hike they take is in a beautiful area with a lot of mining history—not far from where Pete and Cathy meet in the free short story *Together in Alaska*. It's an easy hike. If they can get there.

I hope you enjoy Mark and Madeline's story.

"*I* can't believe he left!" Madeline McGuire swallowed hard as she struggled to hold back the tears that threatened to start again.

Her friend Jemma glanced around the restaurant. "You may want to say *my contractor*. Everyone within hearing range, and that seems to be quite a few people right now, thinks your man just left you."

Madeline glanced around her and groaned. Half of the restaurant was actively watching them, while the other half was still looking at their food but obviously waiting to hear what she'd say next. "Great!" she whispered. Just what she needed. Everyone in the small town of Palmer, Alaska, thought she was brokenhearted. In a louder voice, she said, "My contractor left the state with my money and my house half-built."

The people nodded knowingly and returned to their meal.

"Nice touch there. What are you going to do? Are you going to hire a lawyer to go after him?"

Madeline picked at the meal in front of her. She usually loved the salads here, but not today. She pushed the plate away and leaned back in her seat. "I don't think I slept at all last night. I technically have a case, but he's out of the state now. It would cost me money to go after him and to prosecute. The process could take a long time, and that money would be better spent on my house."

She rubbed her hand over her eyes. "This has not gone as planned. *Build the house of my dreams*, I thought. Other people do it, so it can't be that hard. Ha. This has been the most intense situation in the last decade of my life." An image of her other major disaster flashed into her mind. Before that, life with her high-school boyfriend, Mark, had been the most intense of her life, but in a good way. Then she'd messed it up.

"Earth to Madeline. You seem to have gone somewhere else."

She nodded. "Remembering someone from my past. The one that got away. The one I *let* get away." She waved her hand to stop the conversation. "But that doesn't solve my house situation."

Jemma leaned forward and rested her elbows on the table with her chin on her fist. "Oh, no. You won't get away with saying that and moving on. Before we dive into the house stuff, I want to know about this awesome man you let get away."

The past rushed in on her. Pain and regret that she had shut out years ago were now sitting at this table with them, probably because her emotions were already high. "My high school sweetheart. I thought we'd be together forever. He joined the military and was shipped out."

"That's sad. Was he killed in action?"

Madeline frowned. "No. I let my family and friends talk me into walking away from him because he would be so far away. They all said I was young, and I needed to be free to live my life, that I shouldn't be encumbered by a long-distance relationship."

"Did you try to reach out to him after that?"

She shook her head. "No. He received a classic Dear John letter from me through email. I never contacted him after that." She sat up straighter. "I can't let myself think about what might have been if only I hadn't pushed Mark O'Connell away."

Jemma looked startled. She slowly said, "I grew up in a lot of different places, but I'm from Tennessee. Are you from Alaska, or were you born Outside and moved here when you were young?"

"Juneau. I was born and raised in the state capital." Shifting gears, she said, "My conclusion about my house, one which came to me just before my alarm went off this morning, is that I need a new contractor. I'm going to have to let my other contractor get away with it. At least for now." She tapped her foot as she thought about her morning. "I told my boss I needed today off, and I've been trying to find a new contractor all morning. It's the summer in Alaska, the prime building season here, and every one I contacted had a full schedule."

Jemma watched her carefully. "You need a contractor you can trust. And you should probably have someone look over the work that was done before to make sure it was all done properly. With my design business, I have seen a lot happen between the time plans are created and move-in day. The problem is that the contractors who are amazing are already working this summer. You may have to wait a few months until one is available."

Madeline closed her eyes and sighed. "Waiting isn't really an option for me. I sold my condo in Anchorage, sure that my new house would be built, and I even added in a time buffer. The woman who bought it has to leave her apartment, so I can't change the agreement. I already checked with her. As of two days from now, I won't have a place to live."

When Jemma was about to speak, she added, "But wait, there's more. My six-year-old niece is living with me for the summer while my sister is away at a graduate school program. We discussed it and thought it would be much better for my sister to focus on her work during the day while I take care of Rosie. Easy, right? I'd have a brand-new house with lots of room." She didn't even try to keep the sarcasm out of her last words.

"Wow. So the house needs to be finished, and you need a place to live in two days." Jemma tapped her fingers on the table, then paused. "You know, I can help with one of those, maybe both."

"If you know of a rental, that isn't going to fix the problem. Well, it would in the short-term, but I've set aside the money I need for the house, and renting for months would take too much of it for me to build now.

Jemma caught the attention of their server, who hurried over. "We need our checks, please." The server glanced around the table at the plates filled with food but nodded and hurried away.

"You've been to my business office, Madeline, the older house across the street from my home that my aunt left me. There are three bedrooms and a bathroom upstairs. You and

Rosie are welcome to have two of the bedrooms for as long as you need them."

Madeline felt the tears welling in her eyes again. She blinked them away. "Thank you." She barely managed to get the words out. After closing her eyes for a moment to gather her thoughts, she opened them again and said, "I'll have the movers put my things in storage this weekend. Are you sure you want to have both a child and me in your business headquarters?"

Jemma laughed. "You apparently have not met my twin nieces. One child would be easy in comparison. I imagine you'll both be away from the house during the day anyway."

"Absolutely. I've enrolled Rosie in summer camp. She's a budding artist, and I found something that would be perfect for her. She'll drive in with me each day, and I'll drop her off. I even have some of the weekends planned out with fun activities." Life was looking up. "Now, I just need to find a contractor who can start the project right away."

"I may have someone who can help you."

"Please tell me it's someone experienced!"

"Very. I'm not sure about his availability."

A glimmer of hope flickered in. "Years of experience?"

Jemma nodded.

A smile started, the first one in a week. "Even if he isn't available, knowing that someone tried to help means a lot."

The checks came, they paid them, and left, with Jemma promising to get back to Madeline with an update in the next few days.

The following Monday, Madeline sat at her desk, trying to

work with the weight of the situation resting on her shoulders. She hadn't found a contractor, at least not one she knew could do quality work. As she rolled her shoulders to relax them, a text arrived from Jemma:

I found the perfect contractor for you. He's just moved to Alaska from out-of-state, so that's why he doesn't have a client list yet. He doesn't have a place to stay, so he's going to be taking the third bedroom in my house if that's okay with you.

You're sure he'll do a good job? Madeline replied.

Her phone chimed with Jemma's return text. *I've met him, and I know his family. I've seen photos of previous houses that he built, and I even called one of the owners. I think you'll be happy with his work.*

Her shoulders relaxed. She answered, *Yes! He can stay there. He can have my room, and I'll share with Rosie if he needs more space.*

I think one room will work nicely, Jemma answered. *He should be there Sunday.*

As long as she'd found someone competent, she didn't care how much room he needed. Having someone pleasant to be around would be a nice bonus if it worked out that way. "I get my house!" She shouted and her assistant hurried into her office.

"Did I hear you right?"

"Yes! A friend found a contractor. You're invited to a Christmas party there. It has to be done by then."

Her assistant grinned. "That's a deal. But how did she find a contractor in the middle of the busy construction season?"

"He's from Outside and just moved here." She did a happy dance in her seat. "Life will be great now!"

~

Mark turned off the highway and pulled over to the side of the road to check his GPS. According to it, Jemma's house should be nearby.

A few minutes later, he found a large, contemporary-style house at that address and across the street sat a charming older home, what Jemma had described as her business headquarters and the place he'd call home for the next couple of months. He'd certainly done worse.

He pulled into the older home's driveway, then got out and walked across the street to ring the doorbell of the newer home.

Jemma pulled the door open. "Mark! You're a day early."

"I didn't have anything to do in Kenai other than visit with my folks and spend another night in Mom's shabby chic nightmare."

Jemma grinned. "I know exactly what you mean. I've seen their guest room. Distressed white furniture and a floral upholstered chair aren't very guy-friendly. *I* don't mind it, but I *like* flowers."

He liked her. His brother had done well marrying into this family.

She pulled the door open wider. "I would invite you in, but I'm on my way out the door to see a client. Let me get you a key, though, so you can come and go whenever you want." She returned a minute later and handed it to him. "I keep food in the kitchen for snacking and for my breakfast while I'm working. Anything in the freezer or sitting out should be fair game. Oh, and you have another roommate."

She said the words she'd neglected to share earlier casually, a little *too* casually.

"Do tell."

"It's your client. With her house unfinished, and her old house sold, I felt like I needed to offer her a place to stay."

Her. If Jemma was trying matchmaking, he was certainly up to the task of ignoring it. His mother had taught her sons from an early age to avoid matchmakers. She thought of herself as the master and had made numerous attempts. Fortunately, she'd left him alone once he'd found Maddie. And being in the Army and then Colorado had meant he hadn't had to deal with it as an adult.

"I think she and her niece, who is staying with her for the summer, should be out of your way most the time." She glanced at her watch. "I'm sorry, but I do have to run. Why don't you come to dinner tonight? Nathaniel, my husband and chef extraordinaire, took Chloe along for the ride and is stopping at the grocery store. He'll be making something delicious." She laughed. "I have no idea what it is, but everything he makes is delicious." She gave a small wave and shut the door.

Mark stood there, staring at the closed door and wondering about the next couple of months. He turned around and went across the street. His potentially quiet refuge had turned into a place with not only a woman who happened to be his new client but also a child. He might have been better off in the shabby chic nightmare.

As he walked up the steps, Jemma called out from a black SUV on the street in front of the house. "Mark! Do you know anything about fixing a leaky kitchen sink?"

"I can at least tell if it's something simple I can fix or if you need a plumber," he shouted back.

"Fair enough. Text me if it needs a plumber or if you need me to pick up any parts on the way home."

With a final wave, she drove off down the road, and Mark walked into his new home. His hopefully peaceful abode.

Madeline pulled into the driveway of Jemma's office, her home for the near future. A black pickup truck had the tailgate down, and among other things in the bed of the truck, there was an open tool chest. Jemma must be having some work done on the house, but she was surprised they'd work on a Saturday.

She'd grab a quick lunch and eat on the front porch so she didn't bother the worker. After moving out of her house and into this one this week, she was grateful for a day with no real commitments. At dinnertime, she would carry her cake across the street to her birthday party. Not that anyone knew it *was* her birthday.

Jemma and Nathaniel had invited her to come for dinner in their beautiful newer home across the street, and she'd said she would bring dessert, which would be the cake she'd made for her birthday. It might be a little odd to make your own birthday cake, but baking helped her relax after a hectic day. She loved her job as the human resources manager for a major cargo company in Anchorage, but that didn't mean there weren't stressful days, and yesterday had been one of those.

Madeline stepped onto the porch, then through the front door into the living room and heard clanking sounds. When she walked into the kitchen, she froze in her tracks. The backside of what appeared to be a well-built man stuck out from underneath the kitchen sink. Plumbers must be working out these days because this was not the rear end she would have expected.

As she admired the view, she noticed the chocolate cake on the counter that she'd made late last night and frosted this morning. And the giant missing wedge of it.

Someone had been eating her cake.

This was Jemma's business address, and she certainly couldn't fault her for having a snack, but that was a really big piece, and that was a big guy under her sink. She turned toward him. "Did you eat my birthday cake?" She said the words with more emphasis and a little louder than she'd intended, but this had her riled.

He jerked upward, she heard a thump, and then "Ouch!" He scooted out, and as he cleared the cupboard, reached up and put his hand on top of his head. Then he sat down and leaned forward, gently touching the spot where he'd apparently smacked it

"Jemma said—" He winced. "That's going to be a knot, but not my first. The construction business can leave you with a few bumps, bruises, and scars."

The plumber's voice somehow sounded familiar. She dismissed the thought because that wasn't possible. She did not know a single plumber in Palmer. In fact, she knew almost no one here. She'd have to make friends once she got settled and hoped Jemma would help with that.

He stood with his back to her and turned on the water at the sink. The plumbing industry was turning out some handsome specimens. Broad shoulders tapered down to a narrow waist.

"Everything works here." He got down on his knees and checked under the sink, feeling around on the pipes. "And everything's dry down here. No more leaky faucet." He stood. "Now what did you say about a birthday cake? Jemma told me that anything in the cupboards or sitting out should be fine for me to snack on. I thought I'd struck the mother lode when I found that cake." He gathered a few tools in his hands and then turned to face her. "I'm sorry if it was your birthday—"

He froze when he saw her.

Over a decade had passed since she'd looked into those eyes, the eyes of the only man she had ever loved. They seemed sadder now, world-weary.

"I must be hallucinating." He reached up and put his hand on the place he'd bumped. "I hit my head harder than I'd realized. I'm sorry, but you look exactly like a girl I knew a long time ago."

"Mark?"

He stared at her. "If you know my name, then I'm not seeing things. Maddie, is that you?" A smile began and grew wider.

She gulped. Here before her stood the man she'd let get away. As she took a step forward, he took a step back, and his expression changed from happiness to anger.

CHAPTER TWO

"*W*hat are *you* doing here?" they both said at the same time.

Mark pointed at her. "You first."

"I'm living here while I wait for my house to be finished."

"I'm a contractor who is staying here while I finish someone's house." He gave her a sideways stare. "The odds of the two of us living here at the same time are astronomical."

Madeline closed her eyes for a moment. There was no way this could be any more embarrassing. Opening her eyes, she sighed. "I told her about my high school sweetheart last week."

A muscle in his jaw twitched. "We've been set up. I'll get my things and be out of here in just a few minutes. I'm sorry that I darkened your doorstep even if it was your temporary one."

Madeline watched him hurry upstairs. For about two minutes, Mark O'Connell had been part of her life again. She ignored the flutter of excitement she'd felt at seeing him again.

He stomped down the stairs with a duffel bag in each hand and headed for the front door. As he did so, she realized that this wasn't just Mark leaving, this was her unfinished house possibly sitting open to the elements for months while she waited for someone else to take the job. And he'd lose a job too. She had to get past this thing with him and hoped he could too.

"Mark! Wait!"

He stopped and turned to face her, silently waiting for her to continue. When she hesitated, he raised one eyebrow.

"Maybe we can be kind to each other. Or at least put up with each other for the time it takes you to finish my house. I'm sorry that I have to ask that, but I have saved every penny that I could for years so I could build this house, and it's about to be a dream that vanishes. And it's also a job for you."

He watched her as she shifted from foot to foot.

"Okay. I'll do it but under one condition. No, make that two conditions."

"Okaaay," she said slowly.

"One," he held up a finger, "I need to have some time to myself every day."

That might be hard with Rosie here, but they'd figure out a way to make it work. "I can agree to that. What's your second condition?"

When he gave her a slow smile, she felt tingles all the way down to her toes. His smile had done that to her from the moment she'd seen him as more than the boy down the street. That boy had been handsome. This man probably broke hearts every time he walked through a room with women in it.

"I get to have another slice of that cake."

She laughed. Maybe they *could* make this work.

He gave her a sideways glance. "Hey, did you say that was your *birthday* cake?"

She shrugged. "I've been invited to have dinner across the street with Jemma and her husband Nathaniel, and I said I would bring dessert. They don't know it's my birthday. The last thing I want is someone giving me a gift when they've invited me for dinner."

He ambled over to the cake. "Maybe you can fill in the empty spot with frosting."

Madeline grinned. "I don't think that would fool anyone if they tried to cut it."

He shook his head. "I've also been invited to dinner. I'll confess to the cake thievery." He looked at her again. "Jemma said your niece would be here with us."

"She's spending a month with me this summer. You remember Sadie, my sister?"

He nodded.

"She got married about eight years ago. They were very much in love, but he was killed in a motorcycle accident."

A pained expression passed over Mark's face. "I'm sorry she had to experience that."

"She's doing okay now. It's been a couple years. She's trying to finish up a master's degree so she can earn more for her family. The classes are all online except for those she has to take in person at the campus each summer. And it would be a lot harder to take her daughter along when she's trying to go to classes and study. Besides, I was going to have a brand-new house, right?"

He grimaced.

"I'll pick her up at the airport tomorrow afternoon." She just hoped her niece's stay in Alaska went better than her house project had.

Mark set his bags on the floor. "There's still a lot of day left. Why don't we run over to your home-to-be so I can look around? I need to see what has been done and to understand your vision for the house. We'll find out if we can make a quality house with everything you want for your price."

Madeline's face lit up. It nudged a little something in his heart, but he blocked it. He had needed her to help him survive boot camp, and she'd casually walked away without looking back. Then he'd shipped out, and things had gotten even worse. He had to harden his heart to her now, do the project as he had agreed to, and get out of here.

Harsher than he'd intended to be, he said, "Let's get going then, Maddie."

She looked startled, but gave him a single nod, picked up her purse, and headed for the door. "It isn't far from here."

He set the tools he'd used back into his toolbox, closed it up, and slammed shut the tailgate of his pickup truck while she climbed into the front passenger seat. When he got behind the wheel, he glanced over at her and saw her sitting ramrod straight. She had definitely gotten the message. She barely moved a muscle as they made the ten-minute drive to her house.

Hair down to her waist had been replaced with a short, flirty cut just below her ears. Her dark brown hair and blue eyes had been pretty to him since he'd noticed her as more than his neighbor on the first day of high school. Her shorter hair made her eyes stand out more. Madeline was even more beautiful than she'd been at eighteen.

As they drove up the gravel driveway, he leaned forward and looked up. Birch trees surrounded the house. While the landscape was pure beauty, he immediately saw problems with the structure. Plywood sheathing covered the outside walls of the building, but only part of it had house wrap. One window was in, but none of the others. It had a haphazard appearance.

When they stepped through the doorway, he became even more concerned. Mark stood in what would be his client's great room and looked skyward. Jemma had sent photos of the house when she'd contacted him about the job, but he hadn't realized the state it had been left in. Seeing it in person showed it to be in far worse condition than he'd realized.

First on the agenda was the roof. He would talk to Jemma about her contacts and see if she knew of a quality roofing company that could come out this week. He hoped that would be simple to accomplish.

Madeline went over to what would be a large window. "The first time I came to the property, a moose was eating right there." She pointed to a spot about twenty feet from where she was standing. "Once she'd moved on, I stood in the middle of the land. I could tell that a second story would give me a view of the mountains and the house would be surrounded by trees. The road to the land is in good shape too." She turned toward him, shaking her head. "Some of the roads around here aren't great in the summer and look like they would be treacherous in the winter."

He'd had plenty of that, both growing up and while in Colorado, so he certainly knew what she meant. "Juneau had its snowy times, didn't it?"

She laughed. "Remember that time the kids in our neighborhood went up and down the street and made snowmen in every yard? We made dozens that day."

He grinned. "My mom brought out those photos recently." He moved closer to her. "Do you ever think about going back to Juneau? My whole family is here, so I don't really want to move back to the Southeast."

She waited so long to reply that he began to wonder if she had focused on the view and stopped listening. "I left my past behind in Juneau. I left teenage mistakes, things that can't be undone, for a fresh start. I moved away to go to college, and my family moved not long after that." She turned around to face the center of the room. "I've never been back."

He must have been one of those youthful mistakes. Oh well, that was okay because he had forged a life for himself too. To break the melancholy mood that seemed to have settled over them, he asked, "Describe your vision for this room."

As expected, she smiled. "This great room ceiling is two stories tall, and there are beams across the ceiling, dark wooden beams that are rustic and Alaskan-looking. There's a stone fireplace in the corner, one that will warm the house on a cold winter day. I'll have comfortable couches and," she gestured to the wall to her right, "a big-screen TV. For romance movies." She gave him a cheeky grin.

"Don't you mean so that you can watch the big game and catch all the plays?"

She laughed. "I'm fairly sports-free." Then she continued her tour.

He followed her into the would-be kitchen and saw at a glance that problems ran deeper than he'd suspected. The previous *contractor*—and he used that word lightly—had started a lot of projects in the house but not finished any of them. Plumbing here had been partly done. Everything in this house was only *partly* done. And, he may not be a plumber, but he'd learned enough about plumbing over the years to be certain that what had been done was not to code. The question was, why did it get built this way? Unless her contractor had known all along that he wasn't going to try to get approval for anything.

"I'll have granite countertops, in a light color, not too dark, with a big island. I enjoy baking cakes," she gave him a glare but with a smile, "so I'd like to have everything accessible for my baking. The cabinets are either a dark wood to match the beams in the other room or white, I haven't decided yet."

He made a mental addition to his list of things that needed to be done. *Go with Maddie to a kitchen store and order kitchen cabinets and countertops.* More time spent alone with her in his truck because his guess was that they would be going all the way to Anchorage. Maybe they could make a day of it and knock out all the errands including tile and countertops in one trip.

She had a blissful expression on her face while she envisioned what must be the island in her kitchen. His client had high-end tastes. He needed to make this dream come to life. He'd have to see if the other contractor still had any of her money and would return it if he did.

CHAPTER THREE

*T*he past hung over them. Madeline could feel the weight of it. She'd coldly broken up with him and hurt him, but she couldn't take the past back. They had both grown up, and they were both fine.

How could they make this job go well? *By starting over.*

She turned to face Mark and put on her best professional smile. "I'm Madeline McGuire, and I understand that you are my new contractor. I've heard good things about you." She extended her hand to him.

Mark lifted an eyebrow but said nothing.

"We have to start over, Mark. This is the only way we can make this work."

Understanding crossed his face. He reached out and shook her hand. "Mark O'Connell. I have references that I can give you if you need to know more about me or my work." He used an official tone of voice that she'd never heard before. She could easily see him in the military when he spoke like that.

As she took his hand, she instantly knew she had miscalculated. She never should have allowed herself to touch this man. Keeping a smile pasted on her face, she pulled her hand away and casually folded her arms.

"References won't be necessary, Mark. It's okay that I call you Mark, correct?"

The man in front of her seemed torn between amusement and hurt. "Mark will do nicely."

"I'm now called Madeline."

"Why don't you tell me about your work? I think I heard something about you being at a cargo company."

"Yes. I started in a junior position and worked my way up to human resources manager."

"Impressive."

It made her heart sing to hear the admiration in his voice. "What about you?"

"I've been building houses since not long after I got out of the military." As she watched, his expression turned darker. *Nice going, Madeline. You reminded him of the past.*

Mark stood. "We need to discuss the financial situation of the project. How much have you given the contractor to this point, and how much do you have left to spend?"

"I have all of the figures at home."

He glanced around the kitchen and the great room beyond it. "I don't understand how the construction loan allowed shoddy work like this."

Madeline gasped. With a hesitant voice, she asked, "Shoddy? I knew it wasn't complete, but I assumed it was quality."

Mark watched her for a moment before replying. "*Shoddy* might be the wrong word. *Incomplete* might be more appropriate, at least from what I can see right now. I haven't had a chance to dig into the actual structure. Let's just say that this man did not do you any favors."

Madeline felt her dream of a beautiful home crumbling. "I saved every penny I could after college. I never went out to lunch. I shopped the sales and used coupons. I made gifts. And I drive an old car, a very old car. My entire focus for years has been on building my dream home, and I wanted it to be debt-free." Memories of her parents losing everything a decade ago flooded in.

"Could your family help you finish the project, and you'd pay them back?"

He must not have heard about what happened. She quietly replied. "Mark, my parents lost their business and their home not too long after you left. I had scholarships and grants and worked my way through college."

He looked at her with compassion in his eyes. "I knew they'd moved, and I knew that meant they'd closed the restaurant, but I didn't realize they'd gone bankrupt. What happened?" He waved his hand in front of himself. "Never mind. We're keeping this on a professional level, so I don't need to know about your family situation."

She watched him. She could pretend they didn't have a romantic past, but that didn't have to undo family memories. "When someone enjoyed eating the food Mom and Dad made, they told them they should open a restaurant. Unfortunately, being a great home cook isn't the same as cooking in a restaurant and running what turned out to be a challenging business."

"Where did they go?"

"They moved to Huntsville, Alabama, after Dad found an IT job there. Remember, the family originally moved to Juneau for an IT position with the state government. Mom and Dad have insisted on paying off all debts associated with their business and are just now starting to see the end of those. My sister certainly can't help. No. I'm on my own here." She said that with finality.

She stood straighter. "I can do this. Be honest with me about everything, Mark." She gestured around them.

He watched her with what she'd have to label admiration. "Let's do this then. You may have to cut back on some of your finishes."

She shook her head. "I don't want to do that. I may sound like a petulant child, but I have scrimped and saved for this. Work up the numbers, and I'll see what I'm willing to do without. Maybe I can leave one of the bathrooms unfinished or something like that but have the main part of the house complete. Does that make sense?"

Mark's expression of admiration deepened. He nodded. "It does. Bathrooms and kitchens are the expensive areas for the most part." He took his phone out of his pocket.

"Let's walk through this house so I can get a clear picture of it in my mind. Then I'll talk to Jemma and see if she knows some subs for us to use. She seems pretty connected to this trade."

Their present situation came to mind. "She found a contractor."

Mark chuckled. "I imagine that was no easy task in Palmer, Alaska, in the summer. There's a short construction window."

She paused and started to reach out to put her hand on his arm to stop him, but pulled it back. She needed rules. The first one had to be to never touch him again.

He must have realized she wasn't behind him because he stopped and faced her.

"Mark, I want to thank you for taking this project on. It's awkward, and I know that. But I also don't know of any other way to get it done this summer."

He stared into her eyes, then pulled his gaze away and looked out one of the holes that would eventually have an actual glass window in it. "You're welcome." He took a deep breath and let it out slowly. "I'll need to measure the window openings and compare them to the already bought windows," he gestured toward a large stack of windows at the side of the room, "to see if there's a reason only one was installed. I can't figure out why the plumbing seems half done either. It's unlikely that your contractor would have done the plumbing. He would have had a subcontractor come in for that."

They toured the rest of the house, Madeline showing him where the downstairs powder room would be and looking out a side door into what would be a heated, two-car garage. Mark went with no hesitation toward the ladder that connected the lower and upper floor—for some reason, her contractor hadn't built stairs—but Madeline's feet moved more slowly the closer she got to it.

Mark went up the ladder, all the while making angry sounds and muttering words she could barely pick up such as "Why no stairs yet?" and "What was he thinking?"

Holding onto the sides of the ladder, she put one foot on a rung, closed her eyes, and started up. When her hands ran out of ladder, she opened her eyes to the plywood covered floor in front of her, crawled out onto it, and stood. Thankfully, Mark had walked into the upstairs family bathroom and didn't see her. A calming breath later, she greeted him when he came out of the bathroom.

"All the plumbing appears to be completed in this bathroom."

She went into her master bedroom and over to the big window, letting out a big sigh when she saw what would be the view from her bed.

"Once again, you went straight to a window." He stood beside her.

"You're right." She sighed. "I could stand here looking at this view all day."

"You chose your land well. I'm surprised no house was built here decades ago."

Hearing his words of praise warmed her heart. "A family owns quite a few acres and decided to sell off a few lots on one side. I have two acres."

He nodded and glanced out that window before walking over to a doorway. "This is a massive walk-in closet."

"I wanted to have lots of room for shoes."

He gave her a glance that was in-between disgusted and amused. "Women and shoes."

She laughed again. "On my off-work hours, I keep it pretty casual." She held up a sneakered foot. "But at work, I dress professionally. I learned years ago that I command more respect in the office as a woman if I look pulled together. I might be able to carry it off better without that if I had a different personality, but I'm a little too relaxed to be the boss without the uniform."

Mark glanced around the room and said, "We'll figure out the shelving later," as he went over to the other doorway, which led to her master bath. This time, he went inside, with her following him. He shook his head when he looked at what would be the location of her shower. "I don't understand, Maddie. I'm sorry, I mean Madeline. The toilet and two sinks are plumbed, but I don't see anything for a shower or tub, and my guess is that you planned for both of those because this room is massive."

Her eyes followed his, and she noticed that he was right. This is what blind trust got her. "I remember when he had the plumber working here, and he showed me some of the things he'd done. I should have paid more attention to the project, but I trusted him."

Mark gave her a long hard look, and she felt uncomfortable under his gaze. "Don't worry. I'll get to the bottom of this, and you will have a quality house when it's done. You can trust *me*." He emphasized the word "me" in a way that twisted her heart.

Once they'd walked through the rest of the upstairs, which included the two smaller bedrooms, Mark returned to the master bedroom. "You chose to put your room here because of the view, am I right?"

"Absolutely. This room has the best views in the house."

Mark checked around the window frame, then stepped back. "As we walked around the rest of the upstairs, I thought that very thing."

He took another step backward, as though he was evaluating the window opening. "Madeline, what do you think about changing this from a large window into French doors opening onto a small deck, a private deck off the master bedroom? When you step out onto the deck, the view will be even more impressive."

Madeline hurried over to the window. When she looked to the left and then to the right, she realized that it would be spectacular. Her heart raced as she thought about being able to step out onto that porch on a July morning and sit down with a cup of coffee. Then her heart sank, and she felt tears starting to well in her eyes. "But Mark, I can't afford to make any additions to the house. You just told me that I can't even afford to do what is already planned." She stood there, wringing her hands.

"It will be much harder to make the addition later, Madeline. Let's focus on the structure of the house right now, and we'll get into the finishing touches later. Your idea about leaving a bathroom unfinished may be the right answer. But it's too early to know."

His idea was so fabulous that she could see herself outside standing on the deck. "Okay, I can see your vision for this. Let's do it." With a determined nod of her head, she was in. "You're good at this, Mark O'Connell. You know that?"

"Yes, ma'am. I worked very hard to become good at this."

She was going to have a fine contractor and keep everything professional. That was the only way for this to succeed. "Let's go downstairs now."

She dreaded the climb down. She especially disliked having to climb over the top of the ladder and find the first rung with her foot. As they walked toward the ladder, her following Mark, she wished he had a reason to be outside while she climbed down.

He stepped over the ladder, effortlessly moved down the rungs, and soon stood in the great room, studying the construction details.

Madeline swallowed hard, said a prayer, and dropped onto all fours so she could back up to the ladder and scoot over the top and onto it. She'd come up here a few weeks ago. After more than an hour, she'd figured out this system and gotten herself down the ladder. Maybe Mark wouldn't look up while she did it.

"Madeline, what are you doing?"

Heart racing, her feet found the first rung. Hoping for a strong voice, she said, "Coming down the ladder," but something close to a whisper came out instead.

Three rungs down, she gasped when strong hands grabbed her from each side and lifted her to the floor in front of him.

"Thank you," she said in a raspy voice. She could feel his warmth from a foot away. Maybe it was her getting flushed from his nearness.

"You should have said something."

She took a step backward, and her knees buckled. He grabbed her by the elbows and held her up, his touch searing her. She fought a sigh when she looked up. He'd become such a handsome man. She stepped back again, this time more stable, but grateful she didn't have to speak. Good thing this was a business-only relationship.

Mark seemed unaffected by the moment. He walked into the center of the room and said in his usual even tones, "We'll figure out this construction project when we get home."

Then reality hit her. Not only was he a man she had loved with all her heart and now the contractor helping salvage her dream, he was also her roommate.

CHAPTER FOUR

hey drove in silence back to their temporary home. She couldn't believe that Jemma had figured out how to find Mark so she could get them together. It certainly wasn't the first time someone had tried to play matchmaker with her—single people in their later thirties were open targets for that—but it was the first time anyone had done such a thorough job.

Her friend had good intentions, but she simply didn't understand the amount of pain surrounding this relationship. Or rather the end of it.

As they walked inside, Mark said, "Pull out all of the paperwork you have, all of the contracts and any receipts, and make a list of the money that you've paid thus far and what was supposed to be accomplished for that money."

She went over to a plastic bin and popped it open. "This is my house box. All of my ideas are in here, everything that I want the house to become. Anything to do with the financial and the construction side of the job is also in here." She pulled out a file folder, which she handed to him.

Mark flipped through it from beginning to end. "The scope of the project is clearly laid out here, and the contract seems solid. He owes you the money for the work that was not completed. Do you know where he went?"

"He said he had a bigger project in Seattle and left with no warning."

"It's all hopeful, of course, but we may be able to get some of your money back. No offense, but some men think they can take advantage of women."

She squared her shoulders. "Excuse me?"

"Don't get your hackles up." He softened his voice. "Madeline, he did get away with it."

She opened her mouth to defend herself, then realized she didn't have anything to say in her defense. "You're right. I should have known. Why didn't I notice this sooner?"

He shrugged. "Maybe because you don't know anything about construction?" He gave a hesitant smile.

She laughed. "Point taken."

Her phone rang and she took it out of her purse. "It's my sister, so I need to take it. She answered the call as she started up the stairs toward her room at the end of the upstairs hall.

To her sister, she said, "Let me get comfortable." As she closed the door to her room, she said, "Okay, I'm in a private spot now."

"From who?"

"That's right. I haven't talked to you in a couple days. You know that house that I get to stay in for free?" Before her sister could answer, she continued, "The catch is that my contractor is also staying here."

"Oh, well, he's probably twice your age, happily married, and has three kids."

"No. It's Mark O'Connell."

"What?" Her sister shrieked so loudly that Madeline had to hold the phone away from her ear. In a more normal voice, Sadie said, "What is *he* doing there? More important than that: are you interested?"

Madeline grinned. Sadie had a way of making her smile even when life threw her a curveball. "My friend Jemma somehow knew him. He just moved back to Alaska."

"You're kidding! But that still doesn't explain *why* she knew to try to find him in the first place."

"I told her about a long-ago relationship mistake and gave the boy's name. She put the pieces together."

"Does he have a clue about what he's doing on a construction site?

"He actually has years of experience and really seems to know what he's doing. We walked my job site. Sadie, my other contractor ripped me off big time. I might not be able to finish building the house." Tears filled her eyes, and she sniffed. "Mark seems to want to help."

"Oh, I am so sorry, Maddie. You've saved for this for years. What are you going to do if you don't have enough money?"

Madeline explained what she'd proposed about the bathroom. "I just hope that will be enough." She sat down on the edge of the bed. "The good news is that I'll at least have a buffer between Mark and me here in the house. I can't wait to see Rosie."

After a moment's hesitation, her sister spoke. "About that. I thought I was calling you with good news because taking care of a six-year-old for a month is no easy task, let me tell you. I discovered that the school that I go to for my on-site classes sponsors a summer program for kids. Because I'm a student at the school, it's close to free. I can be a mom *and* a good student."

Her sister's words washed through her. "So—"

"You're going to be alone in the house with Mark O'Connell. Did he turn out ugly? That seems kind of impossible because he was one fine specimen of a teenager. At least as I remember."

There Sadie went again, making her smile. "It may be hard to imagine, but he's even better looking now. And before you ask, he doesn't seem to be married or otherwise involved with anyone because he moved back to Alaska by himself and hasn't mentioned anyone following him here."

Madeline heard her niece say, "Don't forget to tell Aunt Madeline hello!"

"I heard her. Tell her hello back."

After Sadie had done that, Madeline ended the call by saying, "If I think of anything, sis, I'll call you."

Madeline sat on the edge of her bed, wondering what she would do. When she went back downstairs, she found Mark sitting at the kitchen table with her folder full of papers in front of him, a calculator beside that, and a pad of paper in front of him that he was scribbling on.

Waving toward the chair beside him, he said, "Please sit here. I've had a hard look at the numbers." He set the pad of paper between them and tapped it with the pen. "I have to caution you that this is based on that one brief walk through your house. We may find something else as we're working. I hope not, though. As it stands, and from what I can tell even with some research online for the pricing here in this area, you've overpaid him for the work he completed."

"Overpaid by how much?"

"It's still early, so I don't want to get into this too far, but I think it's safe to say the word *thousands*."

Several moments passed in silence. After going over the column of numbers, she spoke. "I'm glad you're on the job now, Mark." Pulling her eyes away from the numbers, she turned toward him and instantly regretted it. His face was only inches from hers. That wouldn't do. Quickly pushing the chair back, she stood. "My sister had good news—well, good for her, maybe not so good for our situation."

"Okay. Will I like this news?"

"Nope. A special program at Sadie's school is making it possible for Rosie to stay with her this summer. She doesn't need to send her to me."

"That's good, right? You won't need to have her here . . ." His words trailed off, and then he cleared his throat. "She won't be here. We'll be alone."

"Correct." And Madeline didn't know what to do about that. She glanced at her watch. "I need to make a run to the grocery store. Is there anything you want?"

"I'll eat almost anything. Remember: I was in the Army. But, as delicious as that cake was, I would like to have a better breakfast than leftover cake to start the day. Please get some of those breakfast burritos or breakfast bowls or something like that. For lunch, I'll need a sandwich. If you could get turkey or ham, cheese, and bread, maybe some apples and chips, that would make a decent lunch. Maybe with cake? I'll pay you when you get back."

"Tonight, we're having chocolate cake for dessert. What's left of it, that is." She grinned. "I think you're going to go have to go without cake for lunch." She grabbed her purse and left.

Madeline was dangerous for his heart when she was playful. He'd made it clear that they were on a professional basis, but he needed to keep reminding himself of the pain she'd caused him. He pushed away those thoughts for now. It would be a long month or few months here.

Looking through the data she'd handed him didn't leave him optimistic. The numbers didn't lie. Madeline could no longer afford to build the home of her dreams. She had the shell of a house—if you could even call it that with the roof missing. He might have been able to walk away from a stranger with a problem like this. Simply tell them that they no longer had the money for the project. But he couldn't walk away from Maddie.

Even with the way things had ended, they'd been friends since they were toddlers. He stood and walked across the room. When he turned, he eyed her chocolate cake for a moment, wondering how much more trouble he could get in since he'd already taken a big wedge out of it.

He decided he didn't want that much trouble.

He needed to push forward with this project. If there was one thing he'd learned in the military, it was to follow a plan. That had served him well in the construction business too. Once he had a starting point, he just needed the next steps.

He took out his phone, but when he was about to push the button to call his dad, he paused. His parents had been very angry when Maddie had broken it off. His finger moved to another speed dial button, his brother Adam's. He had a way of cutting through a situation to figure it out. After asking if his brother had time to talk, he dove into the subject. "Your sister-in-law Jemma is playing matchmaker."

Silence greeted him. His brother cleared his throat but didn't say anything.

"You're part of this, aren't you?" He couldn't believe his brother would be in on a matchmaking scheme. Especially *this* one.

"She asked me before she went ahead with it. But I didn't know what her scheme was at the time. I only knew that she had talked to Maddie and realized that she had known you in the past. She said Maddie seemed sad about the end of your relationship."

Mark slammed his fist on the table. "Maddie shouldn't have done it."

"You're right. But you were both kids. You just grew up fast because you were in the military."

"Truer words were never spoken." The papers spread across the small kitchen table caught his eye. "Let's not talk about the past. I almost forgot why I called. I am in a house across from the one where Jemma and Nathaniel live."

"I lived there while Holly helped me find my house. Isn't it Jemma's business address now?"

"Yes. That's mostly downstairs, especially in the former dining room. She contacted me and said she had a friend who was building a house. The contractor left the state with a big chunk of her money and with the house unfinished. Would I take the job on? I'd just arrived in Alaska, so I had plenty of time to take it on. And I was living at Mom and Dad's."

Adam sighed. "In the guest room. I know how that is."

"Once I arrived and learned who the job was for, I figured I'd get it done as quickly as possible and walk away. But Adam . . ."

"Is she getting to you?"

"I don't even want to go into that right now. I have other problems. Maddie's project is riddled with problems. It's a potential money pit. Plumbing half done. No electrical, because there's no roof or windows. Well, there's one window in, and I don't know if there is a problem that caused the window installation to stop or if the job itself just ended mid-install."

"You can handle all of that. Is the problem that it's for her?"

"Honestly, yes, but no. The contractor took so much of her house building budget that she can no longer finish the house properly. With labor for all of the subcontractors and materials, I'm way over budget here. I might be able to walk away from another job when there wasn't a budget to finish it, but this is Maddie."

"Now I'm angry about this too." Mark heard a change in his brother's voice. "She was like a little sister to me growing up. We can't let that guy win, and that's what will happen if you have to leave this unfinished."

Mark had hoped that Adam would see the situation as he did. "How can we help her?"

"Let me think about this. You can do the electrical."

"Yes, but I can't do the whole construction project by myself."

"What else do you need?"

Mark went over the job in his head. "Off the top: a roofer, windows installed, drywall, and someone to sand and finish the floors. Maddie's specs show that she wanted wood flooring finished in place. Tile. Painting. Picture a house-to-be with exterior walls and nothing else."

Silence greeted him again.

He heard rustling sounds on the other end. "It's summer

break from the university, and I'm not teaching a class this summer, so I can help almost every day. We were planning to go away for a week in July, but I'm sure I can talk Holly into waiting until later. Is it basic plumbing that's needed or something an actual plumber has to do? I can do the basic stuff."

"Not all basic. We need a plumber to put in the lines for a shower and tub and more."

"Let me call you back in a few minutes. I have an idea about some of this. Don't give up hope, Mark. We'll make this work."

While he waited for his brother to call, Mark ran the numbers one more time, hoping for a better answer. They added up exactly as they had the last time. When the phone rang, he grabbed it.

"I think I have found a solution."

"And that miracle would be?"

"You haven't been in Palmer long enough to know this, but I dug into it, and there are no building codes."

"That's why the contractor had only half done parts of the house. No one was inspecting it at each level of completion."

His brother continued. "The plumber doesn't have to be someone with years of professional plumbing experience."

Mark stood. "I don't want shoddy work in any project I'm doing."

"Calm down, bro. You know that I don't either. What I'm saying is that we only need someone who knows how to do the work. They don't have to be employed by a plumbing company."

He walked over to look out the window over the kitchen sink. "Sorry. You're right, and that does open up new doors. Have you found someone?"

"You may not like it. I know I don't love it when Mom and Dad are in the thick of things—"

Mark groaned. Turning around, he leaned against the kitchen counter. "Dad knows how to plumb."

"Yes, he does. We helped him with many plumbing jobs growing up. Then he'd have a licensed plumber inspect and approve the job. The rest of Maddie's project is pretty easy. You can do the wiring. I can handle the floors. I don't know how many times Dad had us work on a project like that in one of the rentals. And Jack is great with anything even remotely artistic. I think he would be able to tile with no problem. All of us can do the roof."

"As a college professor, you're off for the summer, and Dad's more or less retired with his income from rentals, but the rest of our brothers have to work."

"I just called everyone, and they're all in on this. And they're all pretty ticked that the builder took Maddie's money. I hope he never runs into one of us in a dark alley."

Mark chuckled.

"Andy had planned to take time off in July. He said that he can work on his computer in the evenings when he has to get a job done. He'll be there to help where needed." A ping noise sounded on Adam's end of the line. "He just sent me a text. He said he'll be at your place tonight. He's offered to stay with you in the house for the next week or two and be the barrier between you and Maddie."

A feeling of relief rushed through Mark. "Being alone with Maddie in this house would have been next to impossible. Having Andy here will change everything. Thank you!"

After a momentary pause, Adam said, "Are you sure you don't want to fix what's going on with you and Maddie? She never married either."

The old anger stirred in Mark. He'd done his best to forgive, and most of the time, he felt like he'd done that. His emotions were on the surface right now, though. "I'm sure. But you know that I'll have the same problem with this house when Andy leaves."

"No, you won't. Jack will try to finish up his planned photo shoots, so he can be your buffer. If not, Noah will be there whenever his flight schedule makes that possible. We'll make sure someone is there every night for the entire project. We'll take care of you. And we'll help Maddie."

His family was close, but this was beyond anything he would have imagined. Choking up, he said, "Thank you."

"Mom and Dad will be there in a couple days in their motor home and will stay on the property, so they get a vacation at the same time. You know, bro, it may be hard to keep Mom out of the decorating."

Mark laughed at that. "I haven't spent too much time with grown-up Maddie, but I can tell that she has a mind of her own. She has a box filled with ideas for decorating this house. I think Mom would have a struggle on her hands if she tried to insist on any of her own decorating ideas."

Adam joined in the laughter. "You may be right. But knowing Mom, she'd love to go through that box with her." A ping sounded in the distance again. "Andy's on his way." Another ping sounded. "And Jack confirms that he will head up to your place when he finishes the photo shoot he's doing. He says that should be in a week, maybe two. I have a call coming in now from Dad. You know he refuses to text. I'll give you an update later."

"Thank you for everything. I'm sure Maddie will be happy with the results."

"Maybe not as happy about being overrun by O'Connells." Adam's voice carried laughter.

"I just hope Mom treats her well."

Silence greeted him. "Mom took the breakup worse than the rest of us. She'd loved Maddie like one of her own, as she would a daughter-in-law."

"Yeah. We'll see how it goes."

"Jemma mentioned her as Madeline when she talked to me. You may need to call her Madeline now."

"You're right, but spending time together doing the walk-through of her house-to-be reminded me so much of the past that I haven't been able to call her anything but Maddie since, at least in my mind. She's just *Maddie*. I'll try to get my mouth to cooperate."

They hung up with Adam saying he'd be in touch.

Madeline pushed her grocery cart over to the freezer section and scanned it, looking for what Mark had asked her to buy. *She was buying breakfast for Mark O'Connell.* What a strange twist in her life. She reached for a package of frozen breakfast burritos, put it in the cart, then grabbed a couple of other frozen breakfasts.

She remembered that he loved orange juice with breakfast. He'd mentioned it more than once when his mom hadn't restocked his supply. Wheeling the cart over to the refrigerated section of the store, she debated about buying it for him. Would he see it as a nice treat or strange for his old girlfriend to buy him something she remembered from more than a decade earlier?

Realizing she was overthinking a beverage purchase, she

grabbed a bottle and added it to her cart, picking up a bottle of apple juice for herself. Then she finished up her shopping and started for her temporary home. It might be very temporary if Mark couldn't figure out a way to get a roof on her new house and finish the most important parts of the interior before winter. She'd have to sell it unfinished, rent a place, and save to start over on construction in a few years.

Driving, she thought over her recent lunch conversation with Jemma. Not knowing her words would significantly impact her life meant she hadn't committed them to memory, but she didn't remember saying anything more than his name and that she'd come from Juneau.

It didn't really matter. She and Mark now shared living quarters. That would be a challenge in itself. If—and that was a big *if*—he found a way to salvage her house project.

Half an hour later, Maddie walked in the front door of Jemma's business headquarters, carrying a couple of bags of groceries and wearing what she knew was a dejected expression.

CHAPTER FIVE

*M*adeline stood in the kitchen's doorway and stared at Mark for a moment longer than she should. He had been handsome when she'd last seen him at eighteen. He had a rugged edge to him now that he hadn't had then. He'd had an innocence in the past, and that had been lost. But it seemed that something had also been gained because the man who stood before her had confidence that the boy had lacked.

When Mark glanced up at her and quirked an eyebrow, she turned away. "I think I got everything you asked for." After taking a deep breath, she added, "And I bought some orange juice."

"Thanks! I love orange juice with breakfast." The excitement in his voice brought a smile to her face. Then she remembered why he was there in the first place. *Jemma and her matchmaking.*

She'd gone over the situation in her mind as she'd driven to and from the grocery store. "Mark, I'm sorry we're in the middle of this set-up. I still can't figure out how Jemma did it."

"I knew she'd played matchmaker the second I saw you."

"But how did she manage this? She and I were talking about our pasts, and I mentioned someone named Mark O'Connell. That's it. There was no long, dragged-out conversation."

He watched her with an odd expression on his face.

She might have opened herself up more than she'd meant to with what she'd just said. Why would she be talking to Jemma about someone who didn't matter to her?

To divert his attention, she continued because these wounds needed to be buried forever. "She asked where I was from, and I said Juneau."

"Jemma's sister, Holly, is married to Adam."

Shock coursed through her, and she slowly nodded. "I first met Holly at girls'-only dinner at Jemma's house. Their other sister was out of town. I liked Holly, so she became my real estate agent. She sold my old house and helped me find this land. I remember her mentioning her husband's name, but I never knew he was *Adam O'Connell* from Juneau." She stood straight. "Jemma's plan for us to spend time together will be foiled. I'll be at work all day during the week, and you'll be at the building site. We're in control, so Jemma and her matchmaking can be easily ignored."

He gave a slow nod. "I'll be gone every day except Sunday. We'll spend very little time together."

That suited her. She noticed that the papers were still spread out on the table. He hadn't said anything to her about her house, but she had a feeling that the numbers didn't look good.

She turned toward him. "I need you to tell me the truth,

Mark. Will you be able to finish the house? Or—" she closed her eyes for a moment "—did I lose so much money that I need to sell it and let someone else finish *their* house?" She focused on being strong because she did not want to break down in front of this man.

He smiled. He actually had the nerve to smile in the middle of this nightmare.

"I don't see anything humorous about the situation." She turned away and started to stalk away out of the room.

"Maddie, wait! Madeline, I'm sorry."

She stopped and turned to face him, anger oozing out of every pore.

He stepped closer. "I figured it out. We can build your house. And it will be everything you want it to be." He paused. "Let me rephrase that. It can be everything the plans say you wanted it to be. Please don't add anything that costs more money."

Madeline felt her jaw drop. "You told me the preliminary numbers, Mark. I don't understand. Did you find someone who is going to give me a loan? Because you know I don't want any debt. *Please* no debt." She stared up at the ceiling.

"No debt. I do have some special workers coming to help."

"Special? Meaning skilled in some way?" This whole conversation felt out-of-body to her. Why did he now believe they could finish the project when she hadn't had enough money before she went to the grocery store? "Mark, the numbers don't work." She had trusted him, but now she was starting to wonder about his skills as a contractor.

He reached out and put his hands on her shoulders. "Madeline, look at me."

She did as he asked.

"My brothers and my dad are going to help you."

The room started to swirl around her, and she was grateful that Mark had a hold of her. *A bunch of men trying to build a house?* "Your family? That's lovely, Mark, but how can they help build my house?" She closed her eyes for a few seconds, told herself she'd survive, and opened them again.

"Remember all those rental properties we had in Juneau? The five of us grew up doing every possible kind of construction project. And don't get me started on the cleaning when someone moved out!"

She grinned. A glimpse of the boy she'd known had peeked out.

"Dad's the plumber, Andy's great at many things, Adam's volunteered to do the flooring, and we'll all work on your roof." He counted off on his fingers as he went. "Oh, and Jack will do the tiling. Of course, we'll work together to hang drywall, paint, and do anything else that needs to be done."

Not only was she going to get her house, but the men from a family that probably hated her were going to help build it. That just didn't happen in real life. "I appreciate that, Mark, but why would they help *me?*"

"Adam probably put it best. He's the one that got the ball rolling on all of this, so he's definitely the one to thank. He said you were like a little sister to him."

Tears welled up in her eyes. She blinked furiously to try to keep them in. When one slipped out, Mark started to pull her closer, as he would have when they were young. Before she had a chance to figure out if she wanted that, he pulled his hands off her shoulders like they were on fire and took a step back.

"Um, Andy will be here tonight. And he'll stay for the

next week. Mom and Dad are going to come and might be parking an RV on your property—if you don't mind."

She laughed. The weight that had been on her shoulders was flying away. "Mind? I love your parents." She did hope they'd forgiven her for the past, though. Feeling much better about her life, her focus moved away from her house. "I forgot about dinner!" She glanced at her watch. "It's almost time to go across the street to Jemma and Nathaniel's house. I'm just her friend, but I guess she's your sister-in-law. Or is she a sister-in-law once removed because you're not married into her family? How does that work?"

Mark shook his head as though he were trying to process her words as quickly as she was saying them. "I have no idea. That whole thing with close relatives like first cousins, second cousins, and once removed—I can never keep that straight. Let's just say we're related. I've been in Colorado for years, though, so I barely know any of these people. Until today, I'd only met Jemma once, and that was at Adam's wedding to Holly last Christmas."

Madeline picked up the cake and gave Mark a mock glare. "You're going to have to explain this one tonight."

He had the grace to look a little bit embarrassed. "Will it help if I mentioned again that it was delicious?"

"It does. Is that why you took such a big piece?"

He held up two fingers. At her puzzled expression, he said, "That isn't a peace symbol; that's the number two. I had one slice, and it was so good that I had to have another one."

She laughed. What was it about this man that made her smile? There was too much hurt, too much anger, and too many years between them for anything more than these moments. But she'd do her best to get along with him. She had to keep her heart out of it, though, because heartache would be on any path that involved interest in Mark. In fact, she'd probably be better off if she found someone to date him, to completely remove the possibility of her and Mark being together again.

As they walked across the street side by side, Madeline went through her list of friends in her mind and came upon one that might be right for him. Could she, one half of a matchmaking attempt, find someone else for the other half?

Pushing that thought out of her mind for now, she walked up the Montgomery's front steps. Mark rang the doorbell, and they both waited as barking sounds grew closer. Mark took a step back when the sounds came right to the door. It seemed that the man who'd spent years in the military and probably faced danger multiple times was afraid of dogs. She glanced over at him.

"A dog bit me a couple months ago. Fortunately, it was a neighbor's dog, and I was otherwise okay, but it's made me just a little nervous around dogs."

Her former knight had a few chinks in his armor. That might make her like him a little bit more. "You don't need to be concerned about this dog. Chloe is about the sweetest dog you're ever going to meet."

"She mentioned Chloe, and I assumed she was their child."

Madeline grinned. "Golden retriever. Their baby's name is Jennie."

Jemma pulled the door open and looked first at a still grinning Madeline and then at Mark. She'd have to pull Jemma aside and tell her that there was no way on earth this was going to work.

"Come on in!" Smiling widely, Jemma motioned them inside. "Nathaniel has made a quiche, salad, and rolls."

Mark gave the dog a wide berth as he entered the house. Seeming to know she had to win over their guest, Chloe followed him at a distance.

"I'm looking forward to it. I have been eating my own cooking for years, and that was after being in the Army for years. I appreciate homemade meals. And when someone bakes a cake."

Madeline couldn't help laughing at that. As she set the cake down on the massive island in the kitchen, Nathaniel walked over.

"That's, um, a beautiful cake, Madeline."

She glared at Mark.

"The missing wedge is my fault. Well, actually, it's your wife's fault." He cocked his head to the side and glanced over at Jemma.

"Mine?" Jemma pointed at her chest.

"Remember when you told me that I could snack on anything that was in there?"

Jemma gasped. "It hadn't occurred to me that Madeline had made a cake in the short time she'd been there. I didn't even think she'd had time to go to the grocery store." A second later, she asked, "Was it good?"

He chuckled. "I'm not trying to butter her up to make her less annoyed with me, and don't ever tell my mother this, but that was probably the best chocolate cake of my life."

Madeline felt a ridiculous amount of happiness at his words.

"It's also very pretty," Jemma added as she studied the cake. "At least what's left of it is. You're a talented cake decorator, Madeline."

"Baking has always been a stress reliever for me. I'm trying to learn how to decorate what I make. I thought maybe I'd be able to sell some birthday cakes and things like that to people I work with to bring in a little extra cash."

"She didn't tell you that it's her *birthday* cake."

Jemma hugged her. "I didn't know today was your birthday. We need candles." She dug through a drawer in the island then triumphantly held up a package of candles. Eyeing the cake, she added, "It seems a shame to put these in your pretty cake."

Madeline reassured her. "I love the idea."

An alarm on the stove caused Nathaniel to turn around, click it off, then open the oven. "Dinner is ready. And I know that you'll need energy for your work tomorrow, Mark, so I made two quiches: meat lovers and a veggie."

As he set first one and then the other on the counter, Madeline felt her mouth starting to water. This man could cook.

Nathaniel said, "Are you good in the kitchen, Mark?"

"Let's just say that I can cook food I'm willing to eat. But others might not be."

They all laughed, and Jemma herded them over to the dining room table. As they went that direction, the view caught Mark's eye. A wall of glass looked out onto a forest. "This is beautiful, Nathaniel."

"I could picture the view through these windows the moment I found this property. The sweet old lady who lived across the street sold me this portion of her land. Not long after I built the house, she passed away, and her great-niece moved in."

Mark glanced up at the view once again after he was seated at the table. "Could she have been matchmaking? She knew she was going to will the house to Jemma, so maybe she was matching you up."

Jemma and Nathaniel stared at each other. "I know this sounds crazy, but we've never thought of it that way." She reached over and took his hand in hers and gave him a loving expression. "If she did, we're grateful."

At the same time that Madeline put her last bite of quiche in her mouth, a wail went up from upstairs.

Jemma slowly pushed back her chair and stood. "She's at it again. She seems to have a sixth sense for when we're eating dinner."

Nathaniel laughed. "Or when we're at a dramatic point in a movie."

Jemma pointed at him. "Or that." She headed for the stairs. "I'll go see what she needs and hopefully be right back."

Madeline asked, "Can I come?" She glanced over at Mark, hoping he wouldn't also ask for a tour of the upstairs. She needed to talk to Jemma about her matchmaking.

Jemma waved for Madeline to follow. "Sure. I don't know what we'll find."

Madeline followed her friend up the stairs. "I took care of my niece many times when she was a baby. I don't think there are a lot of surprises at this point."

Once Jemma had picked Jennie up and held her close, the tears stopped. Jemma sat in a rocking chair and the baby became sleepier with each back and forth movement.

Madeline decided she should speak to her friend now. "We know you're being a matchmaker."

Jemma grinned. "It's working, right? You were both smiling when you arrived." She brushed her hand over her baby's hair.

"I don't think I fully described the situation with Mark.

He's angry with me about the past, about our breakup. We were smiling because he thought Chloe was your child."

She slowly stood and carried Jennie over to her crib and set her down. When she'd stepped back, she said, "Seriously?"

"Yes. You have no chance of succeeding with this match."

Her friend's smile turned to a frown. "I'm an optimist, so I'll still hope that you two are finally matched."

Mark went over to the window and looked outside, grateful that the long summer days meant he could clearly see the trees. Chloe sat next to him. She did seem nice, so he petted her head and was rewarded by a lick on his hand.

"Jemma's told me very little about you, Mark, other than the fact that you're a contractor who recently moved to the state. Through my brother and his wife, I know that you've been living out of state. Colorado, wasn't it?"

Mark turned toward Nathaniel. Was he trying to find out if he had enough experience to work with Maddie, or was he just curious? Nathaniel put another slice of the meat-lovers quiche onto his own plate and seemed completely unconcerned about anything. Mark decided he was just curious. "I spent five years in Colorado after I served in the Army."

Nathaniel's eyebrows shot up. "I hadn't realized you'd been in the military. Where did you serve?"

"I was stationed in South Korea and Germany."

Mark decided that the meat lovers quiche did look appealing enough to have another slice, so he went back to his seat and put another slice on his plate. "Did you move here from Outside?"

"I did. I always felt attracted to the outdoors, so Alaska

and I clicked from the first moment I arrived." Mark could hear the women laughing, and that seemed to lighten the mood in this room too.

"I know you just moved back to Alaska. What was the draw for Colorado? It's similar to Alaska, but not."

Mark laughed. "It was beautiful, and the people were friendly, but my family wasn't there. When I got out of the military, I had one issue. I didn't want to be crammed together with a bunch of other people all the time. I looked forward to solitude, so I chose to live somewhat remotely in a cabin in the mountains.

Then, in the middle of last winter, I called my parents, and Mom sounded so happy to hear from me that I could hear tears in her voice. Each of my brothers called me that day, from out of the blue. I asked Adam later if it had been a plan, but he said no. They must have all been thinking of me. Soon after, I sold my cabin, loaded everything in a trailer, and drove up the highway to Alaska."

"Holly told us what happened with your mother when you walked in the door."

"Scared me so badly!"

Nathaniel glanced upstairs. "I don't think the women can hear us right now. Are you going to be able to help with Madeline's house?"

Mark leaned forward, to be sure that Maddie couldn't hear him. "There isn't enough money to finish the house. Let me rephrase that. There's enough money to make a shell of a house and to maybe put in the cheapest finishes inside. The lowest-cost cupboards and countertops and flooring. It would be a house, but it wouldn't be the house Maddie wants. And I suspect we would actually have to leave part of the house unfinished even then."

Nathaniel said, "Have you told her? I know she was very excited about having her dream house."

"I talked to my brothers and my dad. We all have construction experience, so we're going to be the free labor. If she only has to buy materials, she can finish the house, and it *will be* her dream house."

"Plumber and everything?"

"Plumber and everything. My family owned rental properties in Juneau, so we grew up doing just about everything. I was an Amy electrician."

Nathaniel grinned. "Count me in. I don't have a lot of actual house building experience, but I'm a quick learner. And I know that my brother-in-law Michael and his brother Johnny have free time in the summer too."

He heard the women laughing at the top of the stairs, and then he saw Maddie coming down the stairs.

"Jemma, I was just starting to tell Mark that I'm happy to offer myself as free labor on Madeline's house," Nathaniel said.

Jemma reached the bottom of the stairs and walked over to her husband. "Why does she need free labor?"

"It's a long story." Madeline explained the situation.

"I know you have ideas for decorating your house, but if you need a decorator or if you want someone to source the right piece of furniture, please let me know. I'm also volunteering my labor for free." Jemma smiled at her friend.

Madeline put her hand on her mouth and looked like she was about to cry. "Thank you."

After Jemma lit the candles on the cake and Maddie blew them out, they each had a slice of cake, then moved over to the couches and sat and talked for a while.

He soon felt his eyelids growing heavy. "I don't think I

can stay awake much longer. I got an early start this morning and drove in from Kenai. Tomorrow will be an early first day on the job site." He looked at his watch. "And my brother should be here any minute." He turned toward Jemma. "I'm sorry. I just realized that I didn't ask if my brother could stay in the third bedroom. I just assumed there was a bed in there and that it would all be fine."

"Of course, he can stay there. If it wasn't for the fact that we have a baby that wakes up and cries in the middle of the night, I would actually let the overflow stay here."

As they walked back across the street with Mark carrying what remained of the cake, exhaustion from the emotions of the day overwhelmed Madeline. With the construction project, discovering Mark O'Connell in the kitchen, and learning that she could actually build her house, it had been a long day.

"Mark, today has been a roller coaster ride. One of the longest days of my life." The longest day being the one when she sent the letter to him. She hadn't slept at all that night.

He covered his mouth as he yawned. "I agree with you one hundred percent." He yawned again. "But I enjoyed being with Jemma and Nathaniel. Adam's fortunate to be part of their family."

She gave a weary nod. "I'm going upstairs." As she trudged up the stairs, her tired legs carrying her to the top, she thought she heard Mark say, "Sleep well."

CHAPTER SIX

Mark watched Maddie walk up the stairs, grateful for the fact that his brother should be here any minute. He was strangely both repelled by and attracted to his teenage love. She had a way of making him smile.

He sat down and picked up a magazine from the table, discovering that it was about home decor. Figuring that a contractor should always be open to learning more about houses, he sat back on the couch and turned to the table of contents, choosing an article on how to achieve rustic elegance, partly because it seemed that might be the look Maddie was going for. But not because he was trying to get on her good side. No. He was trying to be the best contractor he could.

About a half hour later, he heard tires crunching on the gravel driveway and went outside to greet his brother. He didn't want Andy to ring the doorbell and wake up Maddie. Although she'd looked tired enough that he suspected he could use a table saw next to that room right now, and she wouldn't wake up. He remembered her mother had to shout at her to wake her up when she was a kid. As much as he didn't want to feel emotion of any kind around her, he felt sorry for her right now.

He and his brother hugged and slapped each other on the back. When he stepped back, Andy asked, "So what's going on with you and Maddie?" The incredulous expression on his face matched how Mark felt right now.

"It's bizarre, isn't it, bro? I have traveled the world, our families moved, and we both ended up here in a little old house in Palmer."

Andy grabbed a duffel bag off the seat, and they headed for the house. "Adam gave us the bare essentials of the situation. *Why* are you here?"

Mark stopped walking and pointed across the street. "Adam's sister-in-law lives there. She seems to be matchmaking."

He turned to his brother as Andy's eyes grew wide. "Oh, no. Isn't it enough that Mom gets in the middle of our dating world?"

Mark shook his head. "It seems to be a female thing. After the many times that Mom has tried to match each of us up, she accidentally matched Noah. But you know Adam's wife Holly stepped in and finished up the matchmaking for Noah and Rachel."

Andy nodded. "That's true. There are three sisters. If Holly helped with Noah, and Jemma is working on you, that only leaves Bree. I guess she'll give it a shot at some point."

Mark started walking again. "We can stop the matchmaking by stopping this match. And the best way to do that is to give Maddie her house as soon as we can and get out of town."

"And stay as unemotional as possible," Andy added.

Mark hoped that was possible. He and Maddie didn't just have *some* baggage between them, they had a carload of it. Old, well-worn baggage.

When they entered the house, Mark dropped his voice a notch, so they didn't wake her up. "Maddie wants to be called by her full name of Madeline now. She'll always be Maddie in my head, but I've tried to get my mouth to cooperate when I speak her name."

"Got it. Is there anything to eat? I had a sandwich before I left my house, but that was hours ago."

"There's some of the best chocolate cake you've ever had."

"Better than Mom's?"

"Better than anyone's. And I know there are snack foods in the kitchen. Come on." They walked in there, talking about the job and what they'd do the next day.

Mark got up early the next morning and moved about as quietly as he could. He'd forgotten to mention church the night before, but he assumed Maddie would go to one this morning. He poured a glass of orange juice and put one of the frozen breakfasts in the microwave, remembering that he still needed to reimburse her for the food she'd bought.

While he was eating, Andy came downstairs with his hair wet. "We didn't talk about the job last night. Can you fill me in on what we need to do this week? It's a new build, not a remodel, right?"

Mark swallowed his bite of burrito. "Yes. It's framed except for the roof, and there's only a temporary electric drop, the line to a post in the yard, because it hasn't been wired. I plan to get the roof on and windows in this week."

"Excellent. I can help you with those jobs. I know it's too soon for you to rough-in the electrical, but I'll be your assistant then if you need one. Water from an open roof and window openings mixed with electrical would not be a good combination."

Mark picked up his orange juice and took a sip. "I've been thinking about the plan. Mom and Dad are going to be coming in this afternoon. But that's just three of us for the job since Mom does not do construction work. Jemma's husband Nathaniel said he would help. The roof trusses are actually there, so we just need to get them on the house. I would much prefer to use a crane, but I assume those are already booked solid for the building season since it's so short here in Alaska."

Andy took out his phone. "We can do it with a pulley system, but we'll need more help. I'll text Adam. He's in Birchwood, so not far away."

"Okay. That makes it six, maybe seven, because Nathaniel mentioned that his brother-in-law and that man's brother could possibly help too. I think we can get the trusses up, then the sheathing, and roof this baby in the near future. Everyone can meet here tomorrow morning."

When Madeline came downstairs, she found both Mark and a decade-older Andy in her kitchen. In *their* kitchen. The two men were seated at the small kitchen table. Both stood when she entered the room. She did so enjoy being around chivalrous men.

Andy looked from her to his brother and back to her. "It's good to see you, Maddie." He hurried over and pulled her into a hug.

She felt the waterworks starting again. She had always expected this family to be angry with her, and maybe they had been years ago, but they seemed to have forgiven her.

"Thank you," she choked the words out. As he stepped back, she added, "What you and your family are doing for me is nothing short of miraculous." She hoped she'd fully conveyed her gratitude.

"We couldn't let that guy win. There's no way we could let that happen."

Mark got up and put his dishes in the sink. "We'd like to go to church this morning."

She hesitated for a moment. Maybe he wouldn't sit near her. "For the last month, I've driven out here to the small church Jemma goes to." She gave them the address and directions.

"After that, Andy and I will head over to the job site, so I can see exactly what I need to do." He went over to the fridge. "I'll make lunches and take them with us in the ice chest I brought." When he opened it, he said, "Pasta salad?"

"I made that yesterday."

Turning to her with a hopeful expression, he said, "It looks delicious."

That was supposed to be her lunch for the next few days, but she knew she needed to share. "I have more than I can eat today if you'd like to have that for lunch. You and Andy."

He looked over his shoulder at his brother. "Andy, you interested?"

"Of course!"

Mark turned back to her. "Sold!"

"Maybe we can trade. Can I be there while you and Andy go through the house again? I want to know what's going on with it."

He frowned for a second, then said, "Sure," but with less enthusiasm.

"Then we'll make a picnic of it." She put the container with the pasta salad and canned drinks into an ice chest, then packed plates, silverware, and a blanket in a tote bag.

They drove separately—the men in Mark's truck, her in her car—and she squeezed onto the end of a pew beside Jemma. After the service, she visited with Jemma and Holly for a while. Then she drove to her house and was surprised to find the driveway empty. She retrieved the ice chest and tote bag from the trunk and started for the house as Mark stepped out the front door.

He hurried down the stairs. "Let me help you with those."

"I can carry the bag, but I'll let you have the ice chest. Where is your truck?"

"Andy dropped me off and went out to the store. He seemed to need his favorite oatmeal for breakfast tomorrow and fresh fruit."

She raised an eyebrow.

"Most of the O'Connell men can cook well enough to survive—with the exception of Jack—but Andy can actually cook well. I think he would have gone to culinary school if he hadn't been so good with computers. He said he wants this particular oatmeal."

He carried the ice chest, and she brought in the tote as they went into her house.

"I'd planned to have a picnic in the middle of the great room while my imaginary fireplace warmed the room."

"I'm glad you went with imaginary." Sarcasm dripped from his words.

Laughing, she set the tote down in the center of the room. After spreading out the blanket to keep the sawdust and dirt off of them—not that a contractor cared about sawdust—she put the container with their lunch and the rest of the picnic needs in the center of the blanket. "We should probably wait for Andy."

"I'm very hungry, and he should be here any minute. He can fill a plate when he gets here."

"If you're sure." The two of them alone with a picnic seemed a little too intimate for contractor and client, and that's what they were now.

The two of them sat on the blanket at opposite corners, almost like boxers in a ring, but she hoped they stayed civil. She dished up the pasta salad that she'd packed with veggies, cheese, and meat. Then she handed him his plate. Silence hung over them as they ate. It felt uncomfortable, so she struggled to find something to say.

After a few bites, he tapped his fork on his plate. "This is quite good. Thank you for sharing."

She took a sip of her beverage. "I'm glad you're enjoying it." She'd find a cheap way to eat the next few days to make up for this. She squeezed every penny she could get out of her income.

He pointed to the ladder. "I don't remember you having problems with heights."

Madeline's face burned with embarrassment. She set her plate to the side. "It isn't heights. And a gentleman wouldn't mention my little problem."

He scoffed. "Little? You looked like a crab trying to use a ladder."

She raised an eyebrow. "A crab?"

He bent over to demonstrate. "In a hunched-up position with arms and feet reaching for the ladder. Yes, a crab."

She scooted to her left to see the ladder better and pictured her decent. "Maybe I did look like a crab." She shrugged. "I don't know how else to do it, though." She picked up her food again.

"Why ladders if it isn't heights?"

"To bring in money, I strung Christmas lights on houses during my college Christmas break one year. It's hard to believe some of the places people want lights. After one harrowing job that had me place lights all over a life-sized Santa's sleigh on a rooftop, the ladder slipped out from under me as I tried to climb down. I sat on that roof in the cold for a couple of hours before someone came home."

"Phone?"

"With my tools. On the ground. In plain sight. I have avoided ladders since that day. And I may look like a crab when I have to use one." She laughed.

Grinning, he held out his plate for another serving, and she spooned some onto it. "Stairs are the first priority after the roof, windows, and doors."

Mark had always been thoughtful. She leaned toward him and nudged him with her elbow. "And a fireplace. We need to be able to have a real fire."

He grabbed her elbow when she nudged him again. Laughing, he said, "That will be a while."

She tugged on her arm. Looking up at him, she said, "You can let go . . ." Time stopped as they stared into each other's eyes.

A car door slammed. Then Andy yelled, "Are you in the house or outside?"

Mark jumped to his feet. Staring at her, he shouted, "Inside." He hurried to the door and greeted his brother.

What had happened between them? Did she want whatever it was to happen again?

~

The house was so quiet when Madeline got up at six o'clock the next day that she checked the driveway for Mark's truck and didn't see it there. The men had left the house early. That didn't surprise her. Mark had made a point of avoiding her last night.

She fixed a quick breakfast of fruit and yogurt, and then put together a lunch for herself. Until this house was built, she had to watch her money very tightly. In fact, it would be another year or so before she could even consider going out to eat very often. She needed to make sure that everything was done, and that all new home challenges were worked out before she could let down her financial guard.

Her usual commute to work passed quickly as she listened to an audiobook by her favorite author. Managing the human resources department of a cargo company often meant busy days. The workday went by in a blur of activity, but one she enjoyed. It wasn't always fun being the boss, but it came with challenges and rewards that she generally enjoyed. Not to mention the fact that she received an excellent paycheck twice a month.

She wondered if she'd get a call from Mark or Andy about problems at the job site, but it never came. She hoped that meant everything had gone smoothly. Mark had only walked around and through her house-to-be. He hadn't spent enough time there to truly know the state of things.

After work, instead of heading back to her temporary abode, she drove straight toward her future home.

The activity at her house caused her to slam on the brakes and stare upward in shock. Adam and Andy stood on the ground beside what looked to be a pulley system. Mark popped his head up out of the roof between what he'd explained were trusses. There was an almost complete row of them across the roofline now, where it had been bare yesterday.

When she got out of the car, Mrs. O'Connell stepped out of an RV parked to the side of her driveway and walked toward her. "Maddie, it's good to see you." Mark's mother's words were kind in theory but lacked warmth. His brothers had treated her almost as they had growing up. Their mother seemed a little more distant. That drove a knife into her as it reminded her of the pain she'd caused Mark and his family.

There was only one way to be sure about what was going on. "Mrs. O'Connell, I feel like if I ask *you* this, I'll get a straight answer. You know how men are."

The older woman chuckled. "Being completely surrounded by men for decades, yes, I do. What would you like to know, dear?"

"Why all of this?" Madeline gestured at the activity in front of her. "The men have all been kind to me, but I thought you would all be angry." She didn't add that the one woman had been somewhat aloof.

Mrs. O'Connell looked puzzled for just a second and then nodded in a knowing way. "Because of how you broke things off with Mark?"

Madeline nodded. "I thought you would hate me."

The older woman looked thoughtful. "I was angry, probably angry for quite a while. To be honest with you, I'm struggling with it right now. But time passed, and you both grew up. It's none of my business. My sons are all grown men now."

Madeline stared in amazement at the woman she thought would be her mother-in-law. Then she turned to look at the construction taking place. "They've gotten a lot done in one day." The last of the trusses from the stack now rose on a rope fed through the pulley. Mark reappeared and someone else beside him that she didn't recognize, at least not from this distance. She watched as the men worked. They could have been professional construction workers with the way that they moved confidently and as a team.

When the truss was fastened, a cheer went up from the men. A few minutes later, Mark stepped out the front door with a grin on his face. Wow, was that man handsome. She put her hand on the side of her car to support herself when her knees went weak. Mrs. O'Connell glanced over at her, and she ignored the glance. She hoped Mark's mother hadn't guessed the reason for her reaction. Having one matchmaker on the job was more than enough.

A group of men came out the door after Mark. As they walked toward her, she recognized Mark, Andy, Nathaniel, and Jemma's brother-in-law Michael who she'd met when she'd gone with Jemma to a family picnic, but not the fifth man. She hurried over to them. "You've gotten so much done today. Thank you! Thank you!"

The men grinned and clapped each other on the back.

"Madeline, this is my brother, Johnny," Michael said.

"Thank you, Johnny. You don't even know me, and you came to help. I think all of you may have accomplished more in one day than my construction team did in weeks."

Mark's expression grew stormy. She didn't know if he

was angry with her or the former contractor. For her sanity, she chose the contractor. He confirmed that with his words. "You should have had this much accomplished every day, Maddie."

She'd been called Maddie multiple times since arriving here today. Deciding to just let the name go for the duration of this project, she didn't correct him. She wouldn't see most of these people after this anyway.

Nathaniel's phone rang, and he answered it, stepping away from the group as he did so.

A few minutes later, he returned. "Jemma says there's dinner for all of us at our house." Everyone had a happy expression on their face. Everyone except her because she had heard nightmare stories about her good friend's cooking skills. Nathaniel looked over at her and grinned. "She ordered takeout from a barbecue restaurant."

Madeline laughed. "Good news."

Mark raised one eyebrow. "Because?"

Nathaniel said, "My home life's best moments aren't when my wife's in the kitchen."

Mark grinned. "I think I'd better go home and take a shower, or I'll scare the baby."

The men laughed.

Nathaniel said, "You can if you'd like to, but I know for a fact that she's used to being around a bunch of men."

Adam went over to his motorcycle. "I'll see all of you there." He fired up the motorcycle and drove off.

Mrs. O'Connell asked her, "Maddie, could you give us a ride over to the house? We drove the motor home, and didn't tow a car behind us. We may need to go home and get one. I hadn't realized that you were this far into the woods." Madeline knew it wasn't a criticism in any way of her homesite when Mrs. O'Connell looked up at the trees surrounding her property with wonder in her eyes. "It's beautiful here, Maddie. You've done well for yourself."

Madeline looked down and blinked her eyes. "Thank you, ma'am. I loved it the second I saw it. And I would be happy to drive you over to Jemma's." The three of them got into her car and headed that direction.

"So what have you been doing with yourself, Maddie?" Mr. O'Connell asked. "Mark said you were working for a cargo company?"

"Yes, sir. I'm in management for one in Anchorage."

"Two of my boys work for a business someone else owns, and the other three work for themselves. Are you any good at what you do?"

She chuckled. "I like to think so. And they keep promoting me, so they must believe that also."

They drove in silence for a few minutes before he said, "This is a beautiful piece of the state. I can see why you chose to settle here. Mark's been looking for a place to call home for a while. He might like it up here. What do you think, Anita?"

Madeline focused on her driving. She hoped Mr. O'Connell wasn't also matchmaking, because he was going to be just as disappointed as Jemma would be.

His wife answered. "He said he wanted somewhere with a lot of land. To be close to all of us, but not right on top of us. I think my shabby chic guest room has been driving him crazy while he's been staying with us." She chuckled. "He needs more space. I guess they all need space." She sighed. "Maddie, if you ever have children, know in advance that letting them go is the hardest thing you'll ever do." She sighed again.

Madeline pulled into Jemma's business office's driveway. Putting the car in park, she said, "This is the house that Andy and Mark and I are staying in," she put Andy's name first just to make sure it sounded less like she and Mark were alone together, "and the beautiful home across the street is where we're having dinner tonight."

When they stepped out of the car, Mrs. O'Connell said, "I definitely want to see inside your temporary home, and I feel like we should give them a few minutes to get ready for us over there."

Madeline walked toward her home. She knew that his mother had said she'd let her boys go, but she had a feeling she would not be as enthusiastic if one of them moved in with someone to live together. She was extra grateful that she'd chosen the room at the far end of the hall and that Mark was near the stairs. Andy was in the middle, but she and Andy had a brother-sister relationship and always would.

Some of them sat at the table and others on the sofas in Jemma's living room. The room was filled with laughter. Madeline hadn't been part of a group like this in a very long time. It reminded her of growing up in Juneau. Her family had been small, but there had been many gatherings like this with her family and the O'Connells. Everyone had come except Michael who had gone home to be with his pregnant wife. Chloe was in the backyard.

Madeline glanced over at Adam. Her parents had always pushed her toward him. Once he'd married Holly, her mother had even said that Madeline had missed her chance.

Apparently, no one had thought she and Mark would make a good match. Maybe they'd been right. Maybe they'd been wrong. She'd never know.

Jemma came and sat beside her. "You seemed happy and then not. Did something happen today?" She said the words in a low voice, but Madeline still looked around to make sure no one overheard.

"No, I am spending way too much time thinking about the past."

Jemma nodded sympathetically. "I learned when I moved to Alaska that I needed to let the past stay in the past. I can't change a second, a millisecond of it. But I can make the next second better, and the next minute better, and the next hour better. If I add all that up, I can have a future that makes me happy."

As Jemma spoke, Andy sat down beside them. To Madeline's surprise, he said, "That's sound advice, Jemma." He turned toward Madeline. "And I don't mean about you and —" he gestured with his head toward Mark. "I mean about myself. I might be spending a little too much time in the past." As he started to stand, he said, "The woman I'd thought was the love of my life got married last year. She seems blissfully happy, and they have a baby on the way. I can't change that." He walked over toward his brothers, and with every step, he seemed to smile more and more. He turned back toward Jemma, still smiling, and gave her a thumbs up.

She gave Madeline a pointed look. "I'm glad that I was able to make a difference with someone."

Madeline laughed. "I will take your advice to heart. And I know you're right. I don't have access to a time machine, and I can't change what eighteen-year-old Maddie did. But thirty-three -year-old Madeline can certainly build a new life. That's what I'm trying to do. A life without Mark."

Jemma groaned and put her hand on her head. "You didn't hear me. No, let me rephrase that. You heard the words, but you did not *hear* the words. What happened with him is in the past."

A door opened, and Nathaniel walked through the doorway with packages in his arms. "Dinner is here, courtesy of Jemma Montgomery." He gave his wife a wink.

They were such a cute couple. The barbecued beef and chicken that Jemma had ordered were fabulous. They enjoyed it along with coleslaw, potato salad, and rolls. They finished up with chocolate and peach pie—Madeline having a thin slice of each—that Holly had brought over. That woman could make a fabulous pie.

When every bite of food had been eaten, they sat back in their seats, and good-natured conversation flowed around her.

She watched Mark as long as she dared without anyone else or him noticing. Then she wandered over and sat next to Johnny. As she was about to speak with him, a wail went up from upstairs.

Jemma jumped to her feet. "Jennie's at it again. She knows she must make life more interesting when we entertain." She hurried upstairs.

Madeline became concerned when the wailing did not slow down. A frustrated Jemma came down the stairs, holding her screaming infant. "You try holding her, Nathaniel. For some reason, she doesn't want to quiet down. She's got a fresh diaper, she has eaten, and I have walked around and rocked her. Here."

Nathaniel took the baby gracefully.

Madeline enjoyed seeing a man with a baby. Unfortunately, the wailing did not diminish in any way.

Jemma felt her little girl's forehead. "There doesn't seem to be anything wrong with her."

Mrs. O'Connell lifted her chin and looked over at Mark, saying, "Do your thing."

Mark glanced around the room in a way that said he didn't want to do whatever she meant, or he at least didn't want anyone to see him doing it. But after another thirty seconds of a wailing baby, he got up and went across the room to Nathaniel. Holding out his arms, he said, "Let me try."

What was Mrs. O'Connell trying to prove? That her son liked children? If so, Madeline hoped the woman wasn't trying to make the point to *her*.

Mark took the baby and held her against his chest, rubbing her back. The sounds decreased and then stopped, all within less than a minute. The only sound left was the baby gulping as she recovered from sobbing. Madeline could see Jennie's face as her eyes slowly closed and she fell asleep on Mark's shoulder.

Michael blinked and asked, "What just happened here?"

Adam spoke up. "During Mark's time in Colorado, he became known as the baby whisperer. It started—"

Mark glanced at Adam and shook his head a little. "I should probably explain. It started when I was at a friend's house, and the baby was crying. The mother handed me the baby so that she could go in and make it a bottle, and the baby quieted down. The mother stood in the doorway, stunned, holding the still empty bottle in her hand. Word spread, and before I knew it, every time I went to a friend's house and they had a baby, they would have me hold it." He looked around the room. "As you know, guys, when you get to be our age, you have a whole lot of friends with babies."

Laughter went around the room.

"I'm still waiting for babies." Mrs. O'Connell turned toward Holly. "Not that I don't love your little girls. But you waited so long to marry Adam that I didn't get to hold them as babies."

Holly grinned. "I know. We may eventually fix that."

Mrs. O'Connell's eyes sparkled. "That would make me very happy. Maybe a Christmas present?"

Holly laughed. "Probably too soon for that."

"Oh, well. Anyway, having a baby whisperer in the family is a good thing." Mrs. O'Connell turned toward her, and Madeline felt her heart racing as she waited for the words she'd been expecting. "Isn't it true, Maddie?"

Madeline felt her cheeks turn red. "It's always a good thing when a man can get a baby to quiet down. It's a good thing when *anyone* can get a baby to quiet down."

More laughter ensued, and the baby's eyes opened a little bit.

Mark said, "Hush. I can feel her starting to wake up." He gently rubbed her back and started for the stairs. "Let me see if I can get her to go to sleep, and then we can continue."

Nathaniel trailed behind him up the stairs. When she heard no crying and the two men started downstairs without the baby, Madeline knew they'd succeeded.

When she was alone tonight, she would have a lot to think about. Like the image of Mark as a baby whisperer, and what it would have meant if they'd had children.

About fifteen minutes later, Adam stood and said, "I need to get home. I'm not working at the university, but I do need to get a few words in tonight on the book I'm writing. We came separately, so you can stay, Holly, if you'd like."

"No, I think the sitter is going to be ready to get two little girls off her hands."

Soon everyone was leaving. As Madeline was heading toward the O'Connell parents, Johnny stopped her. He said, "I live in the direction that your new house is in. Why don't I drop them off at their RV on my way home?"

"I appreciate that. After working all day in Anchorage, this has been a long day."

Madeline, Andy, and Mark walked across the street together. A mosquito buzzed around her head, and she swatted at it.

Mark chuckled. "One thing I didn't miss in Colorado was the mosquitoes. It wasn't that they didn't have any, but it's a drier climate. It wasn't a mosquito breeding ground like so much of Alaska is."

The men immediately sat in the living room, but Madeline kept going and went up the stairs. She had another early morning with a drive into the city. But she'd enjoyed tonight. Halfway up, she turned around to face the living room and said, "I should have thanked everyone there tonight. What you accomplished with my house was beyond anything I could have hoped for. Thank you." She continued upstairs.

"You're welcome." She recognized Mark's voice, but she'd probably recognize it anywhere.

After work two days later, Madeline drove straight to her new house. She'd like to treat everyone to dinner, but she just didn't have it in her budget. If she could come up with an economical way to do it, she would treat them. As she drove, she went through possibilities in her mind, dismissing each due to cost.

This time, as she came up the driveway, there were more cars, and it seemed as though everyone who had come in those cars was on her roof. It was a beehive of activity up there. Without thinking about it, she automatically searched for Mark among the men, finding him off to the side, surveying the work with a serious expression on his face.

As she watched him, another car arrived. A very pregnant woman slowly maneuvered herself out of it. The pregnant woman walked slowly and carefully over to where Jemma and Holly stood watching the progress.

Both of the women had mentioned their pregnant sister, Bree. Since Bree's husband and brother-in-law had helped earlier, her husband was probably up on the roof right now.

Madeline went over to meet the newcomer and talk to her friends, marveling as she went that everyone involved was stopping by often to check on her house. She hoped they would keep visiting her when it was finished. She'd love to have friends spending time here.

After being introduced to Bree, she asked, "Jemma and Holly, have you been here long?"

Jemma answered. "I came to see how the work was going. I have a few suggestions for decorating if you're interested." She glanced over her shoulder for a second, then leaned forward and dropped her voice a few notches. "Mrs. O'Connell also suggested that she had some ideas. But I've heard stories about her love of flowers and antiques. I've never gotten the impression that that would be your style."

Madeline laughed. "No, I'm going for rustic elegance."

Jemma straightened. "That sounds very nice. Anyway, if you want any suggestions, I'm happy to help."

"I don't have any contribution," Holly said.

Madeline laughed. "You sold my other house, and you helped me find this property. I think you've done your work."

Bree said, "I guess that just leaves me with nothing to contribute. You don't have any children stashed away that need a pediatrician, do you? I have a good bedside manner."

Madeline smiled and shook her head. "No children. Yet." She shrugged. "I've always wanted to have a large family." She looked up at the men on the roof. "The O'Connells always seemed to have so much fun growing up. There were just my sister and I in our family, so we didn't have all of that activity."

Holly turned toward her car, which she had parked off to the side. "I need to get home to my girls. Your house will be beautiful, Madeline." Holly waved when she started her car and began backing up.

They watched the men work on the house for a while. They talked about colors she could paint the exterior.

When Michael peered above the roofline and seemed to be searching for his wife, Bree waved. He grinned and waved back before moving out of sight.

Bree dropped her hand and put it on her stomach, grimacing at the same time. "Ladies, we may have a situation here."

CHAPTER SEVEN

*J*emma's eyes widened, and she said, "You don't mean...?

Bree frowned. "I believe so. I had what I assumed were Braxton Hicks contractions all day long—" She turned toward Madeline, the only woman standing there who hadn't been pregnant. "Those are essentially false labor pains. They cause a lot of women to hurry to the hospital, only to be sent home after being examined. Anyway, this is a case of maybe the physician shouldn't have diagnosed herself." She put her hand on her stomach and winced again. "I think I'm down to about ten minutes apart now. They're coming pretty regularly."

Madeline watched the panic on Jemma's face. "I'm no doctor, but it sounds like we need to get you to a hospital. Am I right?"

Bree nodded. "It's a little bit risky, but I would like to go to the hospital I work at in Anchorage." She looked up at the roof. "I'm afraid to call out to Michael because being startled when you're on a steep roof probably isn't the best thing for longevity."

Think fast. "I'll go tell Mark," Madeline said. "He can somehow get word up to Michael." When Bree winced, Madeline added, "But you should go now. I'll tell Mark to have Michael follow in his car. Maybe one of the O'Connells can drive him to Anchorage if he's freaking out." She paused for a second. "Will he freak out?"

Bree nodded vigorously. "Yes, I believe he will. He's a strong man, a gold miner most summers. But I think he might pass out in the delivery room."

Bree's car was the last one in the driveway. Madeline said, "Get in your car, and Jemma can drive you there. I'll tell Mark."

Madeline walked as quickly as she dared over to Mark, so she didn't alarm anyone. Keeping a calm expression on her face, she nudged her shoulder toward her new friend and said, "Bree is going into labor and headed to delivery in Anchorage. I assume Michael's on the roof."

He leaned back and looked up to the roof. "Yes, he is. He's working close to the edge. Probably not the best time to shout that your wife's in labor."

"That's what we thought. Tell him in a way that he does not fall off the roof from shock. Bree thinks he's going to be pretty emotional about this."

"If she can just wait a few minutes, we can get him down off the roof, and he can drive her to the hospital. There must be one in Palmer, right?"

"To start with, Bree's a doctor and wants to go to the hospital she works at in Anchorage. Second, this baby is coming soon. I don't think that long of a wait is a good idea.

I have never delivered a baby, and I don't want the first time to be today."

Mark's eyes widened with pure panic. "Okay. Tell her to get going."

Bree had reached her car and was slowly lowering herself into the front passenger seat with her sister helping her. Jemma closed the door when her sister was fully inside.

Mark said, "I'll drive Michael to town if he needs me to. I've never delivered a baby, but I had first aid training that included that. It was all hypothetical, of course. Tell them to pull off to the side of the road if she needs help, and I'll pull in behind them to do what I can. I sure hope it doesn't come to that, though."

Motion caught Madeline's attention. Jemma was waving her over, so she hurried to Bree's car. "Why haven't you left?"

Jemma held out the car keys. "You're driving. I lose it every time my sister has a contraction."

Madeline glanced back to Mark. She pointed at the car as she opened the driver's door. He nodded.

When she got behind the wheel, she found Bree in the front seat, panting through a contraction. It seemed too soon for another one. That couldn't be good. She backed out of the driveway and onto the road, driving as fast as she safely could and ignoring the speed limit by about ten miles per hour. "Are you sure you don't want to go to Palmer?"

Jemma nodded emphatically. "It's a much smaller hospital, but I'm sure they could deliver a baby safely, Bree."

Now on the other side of her contraction, Bree said, "That's the direction we have to go right now anyway. I'll decide when we get near the local hospital. I've been there, and I know it's fine. It's just that my doctor and everyone I know in medicine is in Anchorage."

It wasn't long before they arrived there, and Bree pointed toward Anchorage. After a moment's hesitation, Madeline went that direction, going over the speed limit again and hoping they did not get stopped. She drove in silence, but the stress of the moment was palpable in the car.

Jemma called Holly and their parents as soon as Bree chose their destination.

Moments later, Bree pointed toward the radio. "Would you give us some music? I think I could use something else to focus on right now. You know, other than the panic welling inside me that I need to get to the hospital in time and that I'm about to be a mother."

The women laughed, and Madeline reached for the radio. Her old car and Bree's Mercedes had very little in common other than the fact that they both had seats, tires, and a motor. She scrolled through the stations and paused when Bree nodded.

"That sounds like what the baby and I would like right now." Classical music streamed through the car.

After a few minutes, Bree exclaimed, "Okay, the music isn't enough to take my mind off this. Talk. Please!"

Madeline glanced at Jemma in the rearview mirror. "Look at this view from the Knik River bridge! The gray glacial water always seems mysterious to me. And we're near the Palmer Hay Flats. Have you been there, Jemma? I watched muskrats playing in the water there one day."

Jemma continued their stilted conversation. "Yes, I have been there. We went a couple of months ago to watch the migrating ducks."

Bree groaned. "This isn't helping."

After a moment of silence, Jemma said, "That's going to be a beautiful house, Madeline. I don't remember if you ever explained how you decided on that house plan."

An excellent choice for conversation. She could talk about this and not even have to think about it too much, which was a good thing because she was nearing the city, and traffic was about to get heavier. As she drove toward the hospital that Bree had named as being where she worked, Madeline explained her house plans. "I had looked everywhere online, and I finally searched for the words 'rustic,' 'elegant,' and 'house plans.' Believe it or not, this was the first one to pop up. I loved the beams on the ceiling and all of the windows." She continued to describe her decorating ideas.

Jemma interrupted. "We're passing Birchwood now. Holly may beat us to the hospital."

Bree nodded, but said nothing.

No beside-the-busy-highway baby deliveries, please! When they reached the city, Madeline's tension lessened a degree. If she needed to, she could pull into a parking lot, dial 9-1-1, and medical professionals would arrive within minutes.

Then Bree gripped the sides of the seat and began puffing again. The contractions seemed to be getting more intense. Madeline didn't know much about labor and delivery, but she knew that contractions closer together and stronger meant the baby would be here soon. Every time Bree had a contraction, Madeline tensed up.

Jemma announced, "They're coming two minutes apart now. Are they stronger than they were?"

Bree nodded and kept puffing.

Jemma and Madeline cheered when the hospital came into view. Bree sat there without moving. When they drew closer, Bree directed them toward the emergency room door. Jemma jumped out before Madeline had even put the car in park, running into the hospital and returning with a woman pushing a gurney.

Madeline raced around to open Bree's door. "Can you get out?"

Bree gave a single nod. She eased her legs out and then held onto the door frame as she hefted herself up. The gurney arrived as she got to her feet. She climbed onto it, but instead of relaxing as she lay down, she said to the nurse, "Michelle, get me right to delivery. This baby is coming any second." She began panting and gripped the sides of the gurney as it was wheeled away.

"Yes, doctor." The nurse wheeled Bree away, and Jemma followed.

Madeline stood there for a second with her car doors open. When another car pulled up, she hurried around so she could move the car out of the way and park it. There was no way she could drive back to Palmer after all this stress. Besides, she needed to know that everything with mother and baby was okay.

She found out that Holly had arrived first, but she'd gone in with her sisters for the birth. About ten minutes after Madeline pulled into the lot with her pregnant passenger, Mark and Michael hurried down the hallway toward them.

"Is she okay? You should have gotten me so that I could drive her here!" Michael glared at Mark, but Madeline could tell he wasn't angry, just completely stressed out.

"She's in there. They said that you could go in when you arrived. You need to first wash your hands and put on a gown." Michael went the direction that she pointed.

Mark grinned and said, "That man couldn't have driven a wheelbarrow. He was a wreck."

Madeline chuckled.

It seemed like only a few minutes passed before a smiling nurse stepped out and walked over to her and Mark. "Mother and child are doing well, and they would like for you to come back to see them."

Madeline let out a deep breath that she hadn't realized she'd been holding. She stood. "That seems quick. On the drive here, Jemma said she'd been—and I quote—in labor for an unthinkable number of hours."

The nurse laughed. "Let's just say it's a good thing you weren't caught in traffic."

Madeline had started to take a step forward but froze with one foot in the air. As she let it slowly drop to the ground, the nurse's words swirled in her mind. An image of a roadside birth with her delivering the baby made her gasp. *Thank you, God, that I got her here in time.*

As they stepped through the door into Bree's room, Mark put his hand on her shoulder, as any friend might when you were walking through a doorway together, but Mark was no ordinary friend. The warmth of his touch spread from that area through her body. When he pulled his hand away seconds later, she wasn't sure if she should feel relief or disappointment. A glance toward him showed a puzzled expression on his face, making her wonder if he felt the same way.

Bree grinned broadly from her position on the bed. A baby lay cradled beside her. "Peter Michael Kinkaid has arrived. The first baby boy in our family."

Jemma and Holly stood beside their sister, beaming. Michael sat in a chair wearing a loopy grin. Jemma picked up the baby and walked toward him. "Are you sure you don't want to hold your new son?"

Michael leaned back in his chair and waved his hands in front of himself. "No! I might hurt him."

Jemma changed directions and walked over to Madeline. "Would you like to hold him?"

"Let me wash my hands first." She went into the bathroom to do that. When she returned, Madeline held out her arms and took the baby, carefully supporting his head and snuggling him close. A maternal instinct, a feeling unlike any other she'd had, whooshed through her. She had, of course, held her niece right after she was born, but she hadn't felt this then.

After a few minutes of snuggling the baby and marveling at the feelings sweeping through her, she asked Mark if he'd like to hold Peter.

Mark reached out his arms.

Sounding panicked, Michael said, "Are you sure you know how to do that? You seem to be an excellent contractor, but are you good at holding babies?"

Madeline realized at that moment that it wasn't that Michael didn't think he couldn't hold a baby well. He didn't think that men held babies.

The expert that he was, Mark took the baby and held him close, gently rubbing his hand up and down the baby's back as it snuggled next to him. Michael watched with interest. As one minute turned to two, and the baby seemed happy and safe in his arms, Michael's expression changed from one of fear to curiosity.

Mark was more perceptive than Madeline had given him credit for because he walked over toward Michael and asked, "Madeline, would you pull that chair over for me?" He nodded his head in the direction of a chair a few feet away.

She knew where he was going with this. She dragged the

chair over next to Michael, and Mark sat down. The new father looked adoringly at his child. A couple of minutes later, Mark stood and held the baby out toward his father. From where Madeline was standing, she could see Michael's longing expression as he hesitated but reached out for his son. Mark had a calm, in control manner as he gently set the baby in his father's arms. Mark coached him on how to hold an infant safely. Bree wiped tears from her eyes as she watched her husband holding their newborn.

Mark stepped back from them and came over to her. "I think it's time to head home, how about you, Maddie?"

The reality of her situation hit her like a freight train.

CHAPTER EIGHT

*S*he had driven Bree to the hospital in Bree's car. That meant that she was in Anchorage and not near her home in Palmer. Michael had a way to get home.

But she did not.

"Jemma, would you like to ride home with Mark and me?" Jemma could sit between them in the truck. The women could talk about decorating, and the ride would be just fine.

Jemma stared fondly at her new nephew. "No, I'm going to stay in Anchorage tonight. Nathaniel's taking care of our baby, so I'll go to Bree's, and someone in the family can give me a ride back tomorrow."

Her control of this situation was slipping away from her. "But where will you sleep? I know they live in a condo, so there wouldn't be enough room for a guest, would there?"

Bree answered. "It's true that our guestroom has become a nursery, but we added a Murphy bed to Michael's office, and there's the couch. She'll be fine."

Madeline knew when she'd been beaten. She followed

Mark out of the hospital and down to his truck, neither of them saying a word.

This would be a very long drive.

When they got into his truck and sat down, Mark rubbed his hand over his face. "That was a stressful drive into the city. I had to keep talking to the man, trying to distract him, because he was a wreck. He kept saying that he was supposed to drive her. That they had this all planned." He snorted. "His wife had him exactly pegged. I can't imagine what it would have been like if he'd been allowed to drive her. Anchorage is an hour from your house in Palmer!"

"Maybe he would have been okay if she'd gone into labor at their Anchorage condo, and he'd only had to drive the short distance from there to the hospital," Madeline suggested.

"No! That man would have been a danger to everyone on the road if he'd gotten behind the wheel of a vehicle."

Madeline laughed. "I'm just glad it all worked out. You drove him, but put yourself in my place. I was driving a woman who was about to give birth any second. You want stressful?"

She could hear the laughter in his voice as he said, "Let's just say that tonight didn't go as planned."

He started his truck and pulled out of the parking lot.

She'd expected riding with him to be tense, but she was actually enjoying it so far. Maybe too much.

They drove in companionable silence for about ten minutes, then Mark put his hand on his stomach when it growled.

Maddie laughed.

"I'm very hungry. We put in a long day's work on your house, and just when it was time to have dinner, I had to drive a distraught father-to-be to Anchorage. Now, the good news is that we have a lot more restaurants to choose from in a city this size than we do in Palmer. Is stopping to eat okay with you?"

She glanced over at him as though she were trying to sort out the answer herself. "I'm also hungry. But we'll need to go somewhere inexpensive."

Oh. That was the situation. She had been watching her money so tightly that she didn't even eat out. "I don't want you to think of this as charity, Madeline, but I'm very hungry right now, and I am willing to buy dinner."

He could tell she was working on a response to argue with him.

"I would do this for anyone in a similar situation. It has nothing to do with you." He let that thought trail off. *Or our past.*

She settled back in her seat. "Okay, if you're buying, I haven't had a steak in a while."

He burst out laughing. "Not what I expected. But if you're willing to go to a steak restaurant, I am all in. Do you know anything around here? I am completely new to Anchorage, and you work here."

"Let me think about it." After about a minute, she said, "Take the next left. There's a restaurant chain that should serve a good steak."

Mark's stomach growled again. "I hope it isn't far."

Madeline laughed. "Not far at all. We can order an appetizer to take the edge off. Since you're buying."

Mark grinned as he followed her directions.

When they were seated and had placed the order for

drinks and water, they scanned the menu, and Mark considered how to approach this situation with her. They'd been closer than friends, but now they were virtually strangers. He would know very little about most of the people he'd gone to high school with, what happened in their lives, where they'd lived, where they'd gone to college, or anything else beyond high school. Maddie was the same. After they placed their orders, he decided to treat her like any other old friend he hadn't seen since then.

"Why don't you tell me about yourself? Where did you go to college?"

Madeline watched him as though she were trying to figure out if he had some other motivation. When he waited and didn't say anything more, she answered. "I went to college in Washington. I earned a degree in business with a minor in accounting. I wanted to move up in the ranks, so while I was working, I went to school at night and on the weekends, along with some online classes, and earned an MBA."

She had a whole lot more education than he did.

"What about you?"

He stared across the room and then back at her. "I had a lot of training in the Army. I was an interior electrician."

"Why aren't you an electrician now?" Madeline put her hand over her mouth. "I'm sorry, Mark. I don't have any right to pry into your life."

He stared at her. While that might be true, they'd grown up together. He could think of her as an acquaintance. "When I was discharged, I did start out as an electrician. But I quickly learned that I enjoyed the whole building process and grew into the contractor position over a year or so."

"Do you know what happened to Tammy?" Maddie asked about another of their old neighbors.

He told her what he knew, then they spent the rest of the time catching up on people that they both remembered. He was enjoying himself too much, so he was grateful when their meals arrived. True to her word, Maddie had ordered a steak. But she had a salad beside hers, and he had a big baked potato with all of the fixings on it.

They soon finished their main course. When the waiter asked if they would like to have dessert, Maddie cocked her head to the side. "What do you have?"

The man rattled off the desserts. When he got to cheese-cake with fresh strawberry sauce, she stopped him. "Mark, would you like to split a piece of cheesecake?"

"Always."

Maddie added, "But please bring two plates and two forks."

The man looked from one to the other and nodded. He was probably used to a couple sharing a plate and maybe a fork too, but he didn't question her.

When it arrived, Maddie took a bite and slowly slid it off her fork, torturing him with the sensuality of it, but he knew she wasn't trying to do that. She was just savoring her dessert.

He took a bite and could see why. "This is fabulous."

"I know. I'm trying to figure out what's made this one special, so I can duplicate it." She took another bite with a thoughtful expression on her face.

When they finished, he asked, "Can you do it?"

She stared at him blankly for a moment, then said, "Oh, the recipe. I think so. I'll have to test it, though. It may take a few tries. Maybe more than a few."

"Will all of the tries be edible?"

She laughed. "Absolutely. It's just a matter of tweaking it to get it right."

As he handed his credit card to the waiter, he said, "Then do your best. I think everyone on the job site will be happy to work with you on that endeavor."

He was still smiling when they left the restaurant and climbed back into his truck. Minutes later, he pulled back onto the highway that would take them home. The home they *shared*.

A few minutes later, Maddie pointed at a road sign that said, "Arctic Valley Road." "I've skied at the Arctic Valley Ski Area several times since I've lived in Anchorage. It has been my every-so-often splurge."

"You never wanted to go skiing!"

She grinned. "I had to get over the fear of hurtling down a mountain at high speed. I guess I had to grow up to do that."

Maddie had definitely grown up. She was the teenager he remembered, but more.

Headed back down the road toward home, he admired the mountains that followed them on the right side. The length of this particular day was starting to wear on him and he had a tendency to want to take a nap after a big meal. The daylight would help him stay alert. A dark winter night would have made staying awake much more difficult.

Maddie must have felt the same way because, about ten minutes later, her head started to bob a little bit, and she jerked it upright.

Mark said, "I think we'd better talk about something interesting because we both had a long day, and I need to stay focused on the road."

Madeline tried to think of a neutral but compelling subject.

When they reached the overpass for Eagle River, Mark broke the silence, pulling her out of the sleepiness she was starting to slide into again. "You and I need to plan for our daylong shopping trip to Anchorage. We need to buy cabinets, tile, flooring, and more during that one day."

The silence shifted from peaceful to tense.

"Could we just do a lot of this online?"

"You could look online. But I would recommend that you just use that for research to see what you like. Judging from your box full of decorating ideas, though, I suspect you already know exactly what you like."

Madeline chuckled. The man had a way of getting inside her head. He always had.

He glanced over at her, but she avoided his gaze and just listened.

"The problem with looking at a picture of something instead of seeing it in person is that you don't fully know what it looks like and how it handles." He took one hand off the wheel and gestured in the air. "Which finishes do you want on your kitchen cupboards? How does that faucet work? What does that tile look like in person—not on the color of your particular monitor? Do you really like the sparkles on the counter? Or would that get tedious over time?"

Madeline held her hands over her ears. "Okay, okay. I understand now. You're right. I was going to order everything online, but I wouldn't have known if I would like it in person. Of course, being in Alaska, there may be some things that I have no choice but to order sight unseen."

"That's something I'm going to have to get used to. When I had a client with specific tastes, I sent them to Denver, and they found anything they could imagine. Alaska is always a little different in that way, isn't it?"

Maddie sighed. "It is, and I think it always will be. But we'll have a lot better selection in Anchorage than we did in Juneau."

Mark laughed. "Yes, the difference between a small city and a big city will always be huge. But we did okay even in Juneau. You won't have to worry about the job site when I'm off for the day. I'll make sure that the construction is going well and that everyone knows what their jobs are while I'm away."

Madeline chewed her lip as she considered this. "I'm not sure if I can take a whole day off work."

"I'll have to see if the places we need are open on Saturdays."

A warm feeling washed over her. He cared about her needs. Then she realized that he probably cared equally about all of his clients. That's why he was good at his job. "I could take part of a day off—if I needed to."

"You may need to do that."

Their conversation had gone better than she had anticipated. This whole drive had actually gone better than she'd expected. Mark wasn't the boy she grew up with. He'd changed over the years, just as she had. But he still seemed to be someone who was likable. She just needed to keep it to *liking*, because she could never get close to him after what had happened. That still hung over them. One day, they were going to have to talk about it.

By the time Mark pulled into their driveway, Madeline had concluded that she should find someone for Mark to date. As long as he was available, there was something in her that gravitated toward him. She had to assume it was their childhood connection. But that bridge had been burned so severely that it could never be reconstructed.

As she went through the list of people that she knew, one woman stood out from the others. Lydia had also been in the military. Madeline wasn't sure if it had been the Army or another branch of the service, but at least that would give them a starting place. Her friend liked the outdoors, and Madeline knew Mark did too. Now the question was, how could she get the two of them together without either of them suspecting it?

As she got ready for bed, the idea came to her. "It's so obvious." She stared at herself in the mirror with her tooth-brush in one hand. "All I have to do is invite Lydia to the job site."

Everyone she knew had been asking to see her house. She'd give Lydia the first shot at it, and she'd make sure that Mark was going to be on site when her friend arrived. She'd have an excuse to introduce them and mention their common backgrounds. It would be a done deal. Maybe she'd even find an errand for herself to run so she could leave for a while, and they would have to talk to each other. Mark was nothing if not a gentleman, and Lydia could talk to anyone.

Lying in bed that night, she thought over her plan and how she could get Lydia there in a more dressed up way. The only answer seemed to be that they would be going out to eat or to do something. She'd have to spend a small amount on a meal out to make this work. She hoped he wouldn't be suspi-cious about that. Now, she needed a solid plan. That was her last thought as she dropped off to sleep.

Saturday morning, Madeline came downstairs while Mark and Andy were having breakfast. Instead of a business suit, which he'd been surprised at on the first day but gotten used to, she wore faded jeans and a T-shirt, both fitting her in all the right places.

This was one of those moments when he realized she'd grown even more beautiful instead of less. "Do you have something planned for the day, Maddie?" As soon as the words were out of his mouth, he realized that he'd reverted to calling her by her childhood nickname.

As he started to correct himself, she interrupted. "Don't even try to call me Madeline. I've had to give up on that with your family and just go back to Maddie for the first time in more than a decade. It sounded odd to my ears at first, but I'm actually starting to get used to it again." She shook her head, but he could tell it was playful. "And in answer to your first question, after some cleaning here, I'm planning to help on the job site today. There must be something I can do. Right?"

Mark looked at his brother. Maddie on the job site? She'd come after work every day and watched, but this would be all day. Before he couldn't tell her no, his brother stepped in.

"I can use some help with the window installation. Noah and I could use a helper. But I don't think it will take the whole day."

A grin lit up her face. "That's perfect. I thought that after a couple of hours, I might run to the store and pick up supplies to make sandwiches for everyone tomorrow." She stood there with her hands clasped in front of her with a nervous expression on her face. It took Mark a moment to realize why. This would be a big expense for her at a time when she was setting aside every penny.

"That's fine, but can I contribute to it?" He nudged his brother with his elbow.

Andy glanced at Mark and then said, "Yes, can I add to it also?"

Her shoulders relaxed. "Maybe. If one of you could buy drinks, that would be great."

Mark asked, "What about dessert?"

"I'm going to bake a cake."

Mark's mouth started watering. "More of that chocolate? Andy, remember that cake you had the night you arrived? I had a couple slices of it."

Madeline laughed, and it lit up her face. "He had more than a couple slices." She explained what had happened, with him interjecting his defense.

His brother's eyes went from one of them to the other, his expression changing as the conversation went on. That had Mark putting the brakes on himself. They were acting like friends. He could not let that happen. They could be acquaintances, but nothing more. Maddie could never be his friend again. She would wield too much power.

The men left, and she started cleaning. She'd discovered that Mark had a neat streak, but Andy did not. After tidying up, she thought about the day ahead. She needed to do something nice for the crew, and she knew that bringing them lunch would be appreciated. She just had to figure out the most economical way to do that. If she bought a roast, cooked, and sliced it herself, she could make roast beef sandwiches for everyone. That would probably be the least expensive path to a nice meal. And she could find whatever chips were on sale—because there was always some kind on sale—and make a cake.

She started pulling ingredients out of the cupboard. No, she'd make cupcakes. Those would be a lot easier to eat on the job site. She'd make a chocolate and white marble cupcake so it had chocolate for Mark. Peanut butter frosting would make it fun. Spice cupcakes with caramel frosting would be the second flavor and great for those who weren't chocolate fans.

The most important thing she needed to do today was to contact Lydia. She called her friend. "Are you doing anything today?"

"Not anything that can't be moved. Are you finally going to let me see that house of yours?"

Madeline chuckled. "It's still just a shell of a house, but it's getting there. You want to check it out?"

"You know I do! You haven't even given your friends the address so we could sneak by."

"The construction situation is a long story, Lydia. We can talk about it over dinner. If you can go?"

There was a pause for just a moment. "Are we going to eat fast food again? I know that you need to save money, but I don't think I can do that. I usually treat my body better than that."

Madeline had suspected that her friend would say that, so she had a reply ready. "I think we can go out for an inexpensive meal that is actually brought to us at a table."

"Then send me the address and the time, and I'll be there, girl. Do I need to dress up?"

"Let's call it business casual."

"So makeup and socks?"

Lydia could always make her smile. "Yeah. Makeup and jeans. Not that anyone would see a difference if you weren't wearing makeup since you're so pretty."

"Aw. That's sweet of you. Well, I have a bunch to get done this morning if I'm coming to see you. Is construction going well?"

"It is now." They ended the call, and Madeline stood there with her phone in her hand for a few minutes, thinking about the change in construction since Mark had been on the job. He had everything under control, and she had confidence in him. She knew her house would be quality when it was finished. She also knew that she wouldn't be able to afford his services under normal circumstances. The man would do very well in this area building high-end homes. She'd noticed how he carefully managed each step of the process. She hadn't realized what she'd been missing with the first contractor until she'd watched Mark.

She made her cupcakes, and while they cooled, she went through her finances one more time, based on the information that she and Mark had talked about. No matter how many times she did this, the situation did not change. But he had assured her that the house could be constructed for that amount of money.

Madeline grabbed an outfit out of her closet to take with her for her dinner with her friend. That's if Lydia and Mark didn't hit it off right away and go to dinner together. She would certainly be fine with that.

She wrapped the cupcakes in plastic wrap and put them in a lower cupboard she knew Mark had no reason to get into. She figured it was the only way to protect them. Either that or put them in her room, and she really didn't want to sleep with dozens of cupcakes nearby. They might lure her into a midnight snack.

With a sticky note on her dashboard to remind her to stop at the store and buy a roast on the way home, she drove to the homesite. She'd cook the roast tonight. And she'd slice it and frost the cupcakes in the morning before church. She'd have to get up at least an hour early to do that, but it would be worth it to treat everyone to lunch.

When she came home from church, she'd make the sandwiches and then take them over for anyone who was working on the house. At the rate the job was going, she had high hopes of it being finished in the not too distant future. Monday would be her daylong outing with Mark.

Mark felt his phone vibrate in his pocket. He didn't even bother with the volume when he was on the job site, because it was usually too noisy to hear a ring of any kind. Looking at his phone, he saw that it was a text from Maddie.

We don't have to go to Anchorage on a weekend. I'm going to take the week off work so that we can shop and I can help.

He replied *Ok*, then tucked the phone back in his pocket. This was one more aspect of this job that had caught him off guard. He'd expected to dread the idea of a shopping day with Maddie. Instead, he looked forward to it, and that concerned him because he'd wanted to hate her.

Well, maybe.

The eighteen-year-old boy inside him still wanted to be angry with her. The thirty-three-year-old man had learned lessons along the way. One of them taught by her. Family could be allowed to get close. Family was good. You kept other people one notch away so they couldn't hurt you. Now that they wouldn't be shopping next Saturday and would be buying things sooner, he'd be able to make more progress on the job site this week, and that was a very good thing. The progress they'd made this week astounded him, but it was like a tiny grain of sand on a beach compared to what they still had left to accomplish.

Andy walked over to him, wiping his brow with his sleeve. "I've been helping Dad with the plumbing. You can't start the electrical wiring until the windows are in, though. What are your plans?"

Mark groaned. "You won't believe this. I'm having trouble believing it, and I've measured them three times."

"They don't fit?"

"They don't fit. There are holes in the outside of the house. And not one of them exactly corresponds to one of the windows. We can fix most of them fairly easily, it's just more labor. But I'm not even charging her for that."

His brother watched him. "Why not?" When Mark was about to offer him the excuse that she was like a little sister, Andy held his hand up to stop him. "Don't hand me that little sister bit. She was never that to you. You must have mentioned a hundred times, and probably more, how much she'd hurt you. And I don't blame you. You were alone in a strange place, and you got a Dear John letter."

Mark was transported back to that moment. "That was the worst moment of my life. Thank you for bringing it up again." He raised an eyebrow and stared at his brother with an expression he knew would have intimidated anyone beneath him in rank or any of the people working for him, but Andy just stared back.

"Okay, I don't know why I am helping her."

Andy put his hand on his brother's shoulder. "I wondered if it was something like that. You don't even have a clue, do you?"

"Not a single one. I should be starting to build a new life here in Alaska." He gestured toward the under-construction home in front of him. "Instead of that, I'm working for free and trying to piece together a disaster of a build."

"Speaking of that, Adam called me this morning. You must have been making too much noise to hear the phone. I'm not sure why, but I think sometimes he figures that a computer geek's logical mind also works with the law. I have to tell him I don't have a clue every time." He shrugged. "Anyway, he said that they found the man, the former contractor, and I use the word *contractor* loosely, but he's spent all the money. He didn't have another job to do in the Lower Forty-Eight. He just wanted to have fun with his client's cash."

Mark groaned. "One of us is going to have to tell her. It's going to make her feel bad that she chose such a loser."

"I'll do it. Or one of the other brothers. We only have a good history with Maddie. We do not have the Mark history."

Mark stared at the windows in front of him. "I need to figure out the situation with the windows. Mom and Dad should be back soon. Can you help me?"

"Of course. Maybe the two of us will figure it out faster."

Relief surged through Mark. "You're right. Here in this column are the dimensions of the cutouts for the windows, where they're located in this column, and here are the dimensions of the windows that were ordered. The good news is that the windows are high quality."

The two men got to work matching window sizes with window holes.

⁓

As she drove up her driveway, Madeline was amazed at the difference in the house. It had a roof now covered in shingles.

She went over to Mark. "I'm ready to help Andy."

He checked his watch and raised an eyebrow as he looked at her.

"Okay. I get the message. But I did clean our house this morning. Would you rather do that?"

"No, ma'am. You are free to clean anything you want. But I did think I was doing a decent job of maintaining it."

"And so was I. But the dust was building up and the floor needed to be vacuumed. And then there was Andy."

Mark laughed. "Andy was never known as being the neatest of us."

Madeline shrugged. "He's probably very organized with his work."

"Oh, he's organized at home. He knows where everything is. But no one else could figure it out."

She laughed. "I get the message. Do you have anything for me to do after I help Andy with the windows ?"

"I have two possible jobs. How are your arm muscles?"

Madeline pulled her sleeve up so he could see her bicep and flexed. "I don't actually do anything physical outside of the gym. But I do work out after work most weekdays."

"I was just kidding about the muscles. If you can help us get the windows in and just do whatever we ask, that would be great."

"All the windows are going in today?" Madeline looked back at her house, picturing it with windows. It would look like a real house. "When is the siding going up?"

He held up hands. "Whoa. One step at a time. The thing about your windows Maddie is that they aren't all the right size. We will have to make some of them fit by changing the size of the opening."

"My contractor? Is this yet one more thing that went wrong?" She leaned over to look at the stack of windows. "These are good quality, aren't they? I'd rather not install them if they're just going to be bad from the beginning." The anger seeped into her, but she pushed it away. There was no point in being angry. She'd chosen someone who seemed reputable, and she'd checked his references. It wasn't her fault that he'd decided to leave her house half-done and moved Outside.

"Actually, the windows themselves are excellent quality. They didn't even need to be of such high quality, so there's nothing for you to worry about there."

As she started to relax, he added, "On the other hand—"

"Bad news?"

He wavered his hand back and forth. "It just costs a little bit more for us to fix the size of the window openings. It would have been a huge hassle later on, but it's fixable now. We'll start on them soon"

When she went in search of Andy, she found him inside with another man she didn't recognize. When the man looked up at her, she gasped. "Noah? Is that you all grown up?"

The man stood to his feet and pulled her into a bear hug. "You look great, Maddie. You know, I always had a little bit of a crush on you when I was a boy." He winked at her.

She laughed and swatted at his shoulder. "I hear you're an engaged man now. Did you bring your fiancée with you?"

"No. She's visiting her brother in Talkeetna right now."

"Well, I definitely want to meet her sometime. Are you ready to work on the windows?"

"Yes. Let's get started."

Madeline learned a lot as they installed some of the windows, mostly that she needed to work more on her arm muscles at the gym. When Adam arrived, he took over with helping his brothers.

CHAPTER NINE

*M*adeline stood back and looked at the change in her house. The transformation was nothing short of miraculous to her. It had been an empty shell. Well, it was still an empty shell, but now it had a roof with shingles on it and windows, at least those in the front of the house. It wouldn't be too long before it actually looked like a home. And she had Mark O'Connell to thank for that, even if Jemma had brought him back into her life while playing matchmaker.

Speaking of which, one match deserved another.

She felt like rubbing her hands together with glee. Checking her watch, she saw that it would be an hour or two before Lydia arrived.

She had a bounce in her step as she walked over to Mark. There was no reason to be intimidated by her former love. He would soon belong to someone else. She wouldn't have to feel guilty about what she had done when he was happily married to someone else. Maybe with two or three kids. An image that she'd had when she was a teenager of her and

Mark with just such a situation came to mind—married, three children. She'd always thought that she and Mark would make beautiful babies together; his dark hair and eyes combining with her brown hair and blue eyes should make some pretty babies. Shaking that off, she continued toward Mark.

He looked up and saw her. "I'm hoping to get most of the windows installed today. Did you enjoy window installation?"

"Construction is quite physical. You work hard."

He grinned. "Yes, ma'am. I have good news."

She could use some of that. "What is it?"

"With all of the help, I found enough in the budget to have professionals do the drywall taping so you'll have a smooth finish. That's a highly skilled job, so it's not best for amateurs."

Madeline looked around. "What can I do to help this afternoon?"

Mark studied the plans in front of them on his makeshift table. "I think I have all of the jobs assigned. Have you done any construction work at any time in your life?" He hadn't even looked up from the plans.

"Only if you call installing a new bathroom sink *construction*. That and being an expert at rolling paint on the walls would be the sum total of my experience that applies here."

He turned to her and cocked his head to the side. "You installed a new bathroom sink?"

"I did. My little condo was cute, and the previous owner had more or less redone the kitchen before I bought it, but the bathroom was locked in the seventies. I was willing to keep the other fixtures, but that sink had to go. I watched some YouTube videos—a lot of videos—and figured out how to do it." Madeline grinned. "The buyer made my heart happy when she commented on the pretty bathroom."

Mark looked around as though he were trying to come up with something for her to do. "Maddie, there just isn't anything else at this stage. If you can paint, we will definitely have you help at that time. Are you good at making a straight line on the edges or just rolling?"

"I can get a straight line with the best of them. But what do I do right now, Mark? It's my house, and I need to feel like I'm doing something." She heard frustration creeping into her voice and tried to push it away. She didn't want to be the cranky client when they were doing so much for her.

"About the only thing that I can think of, and I doubt that you want to do it, is to pick up all of the construction debris that we're starting to gather around the house. I usually have someone on my crew do that, but they're all busy and volunteers, so I take whatever time they give me for actual construction." He sighed. "These pieces of wood and shingles are both a hazard when you're trying to walk around the job site and slow down productivity because you have to look where you're stepping."

She'd had a picture in her mind of standing shoulder to shoulder with one of the brothers—preferably not Mark—and helping him build her house. Installing a few of the windows had helped, but she knew that Adam was more useful there than she had been. She had wanted to be able to look point to something on her completed house and say she'd helped with it. But she didn't have any experience that applied, and picking up trash would help them do the work they knew how to do. "I can do that. It can be my job every day to clear up all the construction debris."

Mark's jaw dropped. When he gathered himself together,

he said, "Are you sure? This is a crummy job. It's something that would usually be done by a teenager or someone I've just hired on a site and want to see what kind of worker they are. Someone with no experience."

She laughed. "Well, I'm not a teenager, but I think that other than that, I fit the job description." She reached down and picked up a triangle of plywood. When she stood, she held it up. "What do I do with it when I pick it up? Where does it go?"

He pointed to the left. "Let's start a pile of all the wood scraps there. We can burn it all when the job is done. Drop everything else in a different pile so we know what we need to take to the dump. I have a dumpster on the way, but it's been delayed. And you're probably going to want some heavy leather gloves because the job you're doing is deep in the heart of splinter country."

"I don't have any gloves that fit that description, but I can go to the store and get some tonight after I leave here." She started toward the area that he'd pointed at with the piece of wood in her hand.

Mark grabbed her elbow to stop her. She ignored the warmth that flew through her.

"Maddie, I really do think you're going to need those gloves. Run out to get them now. I have a couple of other things you can pick up when you're out, so it won't be a wasted run."

She turned back toward him, and he made a list on a piece of paper from a pad that he must carry with him all the time. He handed it to her, and when she looked it over, she saw that she could get most of it at a local hardware store. She was becoming more and more familiar with this area near her house and thought it would take a little over an hour to finish this.

A few minutes later, she was backing down the driveway and pulling out on the road. A glance at the clock on her dashboard told her that Lydia might arrive before she returned. That could be a disaster. She needed to be taken directly over to Mark and introduced in a glowing but not obviously matchmaking way. She pulled off to the side of the road and called her friend. "Are you on the way over here yet?"

"On my way out the door right now."

"Stop!"

"Okay, you've got my attention now. Is something wrong?"

Lydia was an extrovert in the extreme definition of the word. She would be able to walk on to the site, introduce herself to everyone, and then just kick back and wait for Madeline to return. But that just wouldn't do. "I have to run some errands for the job. Wait about a half hour before you leave. I want to be able to walk you through my house myself." That should do it.

"There's some weeding I need to do in the front yard. It should take just about that amount of time."

Madeline laughed. Weeding was something she avoided at all costs. She'd actually planned to have a natural landscape around her home with a minimal amount of grass and only flowerpots instead of flowers in the ground. "I'll see you then." Madeline started driving, hoping that she didn't have any issues finding the things on the list. She wasn't even sure what some of them were, but she knew that whoever worked at the store would be able to point her in the right direction.

She let out a sigh of relief when she pulled back up in

front of her house ninety-three minutes later, and Lydia's red Honda wasn't there yet. Mark waved Michael over to her car, and the two of them started unloading the things she had in the backseat. With that empty, she popped open the trunk, and they began unloading it. "I have everything on the list." She looked at it again. "The man at the store said they'd put in something extra that electricians would need."

Mark said, "Excellent." When Michael walked away, Mark stood in a way that she would almost have to call nervous. Did he have bad news to give her, or was it just that he was near her?

All he said was, "We're making good progress."

When he seemed about to say more, Lydia's sporty red car zipped up the drive. Mark jumped to the side when her car got just a little too close to him, not that he was ever in danger. Lydia was not a reckless driver, but sometimes she moved quickly.

Her friend parked off to the side and stepped out of the car. With a hand on each hip, she looked up at the house. "Madeline, you're going to have a beautiful house. The property is gorgeous." She glanced over at her and Mark, seeming to notice him for the first time, and gave him an appreciative once-over.

Score one for the matchmaker.

Lydia walked over to them, and Maddie introduced her to Mark. "He's the contractor and a—" she hesitated for a moment as she tried to figure out just how to describe him. "A childhood friend." Yes, that was perfect. "We grew up together on the same street in Juneau."

Lydia put out her hand to shake Mark's. "I'm very pleased to meet you." Her voice had a note of interest.

Madeline reached into her car and pulled out brand-new,

heavy-duty leather gloves. Holding them up, she said, "I'm ready to go to work now, Mark."

Adam stepped out of the house and went around some debris as he walked in their direction. "Do you want to give her the tour of the house, Mark, while I clean up, or should I do it?" She had him cornered because the yard needed to be cleared of debris.

Mark pursed his lips as he seemed to weigh his options. She'd paired the two of them together because she always thought that an introvert and an extrovert could get along well together. One would pick up where the other one left off. He could teach Lydia about quiet moments, and she would teach him how to do well in groups. And it seemed like he needed that very much right now. She wasn't sure if something had happened in the military or it was just who he'd become in the last decade, but he definitely seemed to favor being around family over being around anyone else. Maybe he just didn't want to be with her.

"Why don't you start the tour, Maddie, and I'll join you in a few minutes."

Her brilliant matchmaking went up in smoke. She tucked her new gloves in her back pocket. Pointing toward the house, she said, "The kitchen is over there, and the living room is on the left. The three bedrooms are upstairs. Let's get started."

As soon as they were out of Mark's hearing range, Lydia said, "You have a gorgeous contractor. My goodness. He could have his own TV show." She looked back over her shoulder in his direction for a long glance. Madeline grabbed her elbow to steer her around some plywood scraps. When Lydia looked forward again, she said, "It would be a hit show. I'd watch it, and I think every red-blooded female on Earth would too." She gave a low whistle as they walked up the temporary steps into Madeline's house.

That Lydia found Mark appealing was an understatement. Maddie was doing well on Lydia's side of the match, but she hadn't been able to read Mark very well on the situation.

Madeline walked her friend through the kitchen and around the living area. Stopping in the middle of the room, she pointed to the left and said, "And that's going to be an office. Mark suggested that we put in a closet so that it would technically be a bedroom if I ever want to sell the house." She turned toward her friend. "I can't imagine *ever* wanting to do that. I worked so hard to get it. But it's a good idea. And besides, I like the idea of having more storage on this floor." She looked down at her friend's feet. "I forgot to tell you to wear flat-soled shoes, so I'm glad you happened to put sneakers on."

They went upstairs and Madeline was grateful that Mark had moved the staircase to a higher priority. She gave Lydia a tour, going to her master bedroom last. A larger hole had been cut in the wall for what would become the sliding glass doors leading to her new deck. "This was going to be a regular-sized window. I love the larger one."

Lydia stood at the opening. "You're going to have stunning views from bed."

"That was Mark's suggestion." At her friend's quick glance, she added, "Not that I have a view from bed, but that I should take advantage of the view from this room."

"Nothing is going on between you and the contractor?"

Madeline could honestly answer, "Nothing at all. We knew each other a long time ago, and he happened to move to Alaska at the time when I needed a contractor."

"So you wouldn't mind if I showed a little interest?"

"Nope." Madeline's matchmaking was doing well. Now she just had to make sure that Mark was interested. At that moment, Madeline heard footsteps on the stairs, and Mark's head and shoulders came into view. He said, "I can take over the tour now, Maddie, if you want to go out and get started on the job."

He seemed more resigned to the task than intrigued by it. As she left the room, her friend asked, "Please give me a tour of the upstairs, Mark."

She'd trust that Lydia's natural charm would reel him in.

Madeline glanced back at them as she reached the stairs and saw her friend with her hand on Mark's arm, looking up at him. They made an attractive couple, just as she'd expected.

Why did she hate that?

As she went down the stairs and walked through her house to go outside, she tried to sort out her feelings. Why would the two of them being a couple bother her? It shouldn't. She'd sorted this all out earlier. He needed someone new, so they could both be free from the past. So why did she feel weird about it?

She pulled her gloves out of her pocket and started working on the cleanup project. About ten minutes later, they walked out the door. Lydia came over to her and Mark returned to his work table.

"He gave me a detailed tour, but I couldn't get him interested in anything away from the job site. I asked him if he ever took a break to have lunch off-site, and he mumbled something about not having time to do that." She looked toward Mark with a dreamy expression on her face. "If you could put in a good word for me, I'd appreciate it."

Lydia walked beside her as Madeline gathered more debris off the ground. Tossing it onto the woodpile, Madeline tamped down an emotion that she almost had to label "jealousy." She had no hold on this man. She did when she was eighteen, but she had forfeited that a long time ago. Pasting a smile on her face, she turned to her friend. "I will do that. Let me finish up here, and we can take off. What do you think of my house?"

Her friend grinned. "It's going to be spectacular. I hope you'll have a housewarming and invite all of us."

Madeline laughed. "If you're all okay with a potluck?"

"Girl, we all know how much you have scrimped and saved for this project. I think we'll be happy to chip in with a housewarming party, maybe even bring in a house plant or two."

Madeline laughed. When she finished up working, she took off her gloves and went over to Mark. "I'm going to be heading out now. Unless there's something else that you need for me to do."

He glanced over at Lydia, but it was not with interest. She'd have to sort out the reasons why later, but Madeline was grateful deep in her heart.

CHAPTER TEN

*W*hen she returned from her evening with her friend, she found Mark and Andy in their temporary abode, laughing about something. When Mark turned to her, his eyes were still filled with laughter, and the armor that she had put around her heart shattered into a million pieces.

She couldn't have been more wrong about her heart. Yes, she'd pushed him away, but she hadn't stopped loving him.

But now she seriously doubted there was a way they could ever have a future together. She had hurt the teenage Mark at a time when he needed her, and the man had too many years with that memory to let go of it.

So she gave him a small smile and went into the kitchen and turned on the oven for the roast. She'd go upstairs and read while it cooked, so she'd be out of their way and away from the tug of their laughter, which pulled her closer. She'd have to try to avoid Mark—but she didn't really want to stay away. She wanted to spend every second with him.

She had never found anyone other than him who truly

touched her heart. She thought she had every once in a while, but another date or two later, and she'd realize that they didn't have any chemistry.

As Madeline seasoned the roast, she realized that this project gave her a chance to spend more time with him. She'd make it last, and she would remember this time for the rest of her life.

That was her plan, and it was pitiful. She was even a little bit disappointed in herself, maybe a lot disappointed, that she'd be willing to just hang out near Mark when she could. But there you had it. Before, she'd enjoyed having the barrier between herself and Mark so she didn't have to talk to him. But now she wanted to spend time with him. She'd have to find a way.

Then she remembered Lydia. She'd also have to tell her friend the whole story and that she did want him back.

She shoved the roast in the oven and went upstairs to call Lydia. No matter how she worded it, this would be awkward. *That man I fixed you up with? So sorry. I do want him after all.*

Her friend answered her phone with the words, "Thank you for a fun time today!" As Madeline struggled to find the right words, Lydia continued, "But I've been thinking about Mark. I saw the two of you together. You want him for yourself, don't you?"

Tears welled up in Madeline's eyes. One dropped as she leaned forward. "Yes, I realized tonight that I do. Do you mind if I take him?" She rubbed at her damp eyes with her sleeve.

Lydia laughed. "Honey, he was never mine."

"Thank you! I'm sorry about all of this."

"I'm not. I had a nice evening with a friend. And I do love your house."

Madeline let out a deep sigh. "Thank you!"

"I do have one piece of advice. Show him you're interested."

"I'll do my best to make that happen."

"And one more thing. I always like a pop of red in my decorating scheme. It makes everything come to life."

Madeline grinned. "I'll keep that in mind." They chatted for a few more minutes before hanging up. As she set her phone on her nightstand, she realized she'd solved the situation with Lydia, but not the greatest problem. She had to find a way so that Mark could fall in love with her all over again.

A couple of hours later, Madeline set her book beside her on the bed. She'd chosen a romance, and that would normally hold her attention. But not tonight. She didn't think even the most intense suspense novel ever written could hold her attention tonight. Every once in a while, the laughter between the brothers made its way up the stairs and down the hall. Or maybe it was just through the walls. This was an older house, after all, and insulation had probably been close to nonexistent when it had been built.

It wasn't like she could go somewhere else to get away. Her new house certainly wasn't ready to spend any time in, particularly alone in the dark with no electricity. She checked the time. Instead of getting up early to frost the cupcakes, she could do it now. Besides, it sounded like they were having a lot of fun, and she wasn't exactly having a party up here. Their mood in the room next to the kitchen might elevate hers.

When she was far enough down the stairs to see the living room, she discovered why the laughter had been so loud. Mark and Andy had been joined by Noah and Adam. The four of them sat around playing some kind of card game. She'd never been much of a game player, but she'd venture a guess that it was poker. She had planned to hurry through, but that would be rude now that she wasn't just passing by her fellow roommates.

Noah looked up and said, "I don't know what you're cooking, but it smells fabulous. Can we have a bite when it comes out?" His eager expression made her chuckle.

"I'm cooking a roast, and we're going to have roast beef sandwiches for lunch tomorrow."

He did a fist pump. "Yes! I have tomorrow off. I thought we could get some things done on your house after church. You don't mind if I spend the night on the couch, do you?"

"If you think it's comfortable enough to sleep on, sure."

Noah chuckled. "You don't know the couch I used to have. I'm sure this will be fine."

"In that case, I saw extra sheets and blankets in the linen closet upstairs. Feel free to get them out. Have fun with the game." She continued on to the kitchen, hoping that none of them would come in to check to see what she was doing. She didn't trust them with baked goods after the Mark cake incident. Of course, he had thought it was fair game to eat the cake. But still, she needed these cupcakes for tomorrow, and a group of four men could devour them in a hurry.

She pulled together all of the ingredients and began making the caramel frosting. It would need to cool before she could use it, so it was first. As she stirred the mixture of butter, milk, and sugar at the stove, she decided that she should come up with a plan to find ways to spend more time with Mark. Plans were good. They gave her a sense of security. She took the pan off the stove, and mixed in the powdered sugar and vanilla.

While that cooled, she mixed up the peanut butter frosting. When she'd finished it, she glanced out the kitchen opening and saw the brothers still focused on their game, so she bent down and pulled the cupcakes out of the cupboard and set them on the counter.

Once the marble cupcakes were frosted, she took out a grater and a chocolate bar she'd bought to put a generous amount of grated chocolate over the top. Could you have too much chocolate? She didn't think so. Then she frosted the spice cupcakes and stowed them all securely in the cupboard just minutes before it was time for the roast to come out.

Madeline took it out of the oven, set it on top of the stove, and tested it with a meat thermometer. Perfect. She covered it with foil and put it into the refrigerator. She'd get up early before church and slice it. Maybe one of the guys could help her make the sandwiches. The sound level dropped to silence as she heard voices fading away. They must have gone upstairs to bed. She'd go upstairs too. Turning off the light, she hurried through to the living room as Mark came around the corner.

"Whoa!" He put his hands on her shoulders to steady her, and she looked up into his eyes.

Her heart stopped beating for a second. Then it raced. If only she could be bolder like Lydia, then she might lean forward and kiss him. But she'd never been that way. And with all the baggage between them? That would be a no.

He looked down at her lips, and his mouth turned up in a quirky smile. Reaching out, he rubbed his finger down her nose and held it up. "Peanut butter . . . and it looks like frosting. Have you been baking, Maddie? The bigger question is: do you need a taste tester?"

So much for romance. Mark was only interested in his stomach.

Madeline pushed other thoughts to the side and focused on the moment as it really was, not as she wanted it to be. She'd only humiliate herself and possibly ruin her home's future if she let on for a second that she had any romantic interest in this man.

She stepped back from him and turned toward the kitchen. "I didn't take the time to wash things up yet." She heard his footsteps behind her, and she turned to face him, shaking her finger in the air. "And Mark O'Connell, I need you to promise not to get into the cupcakes. Do I have your promise?"

His eyes lit up. "Cupcakes? Are these for someone else, or will I get to have one of them later?"

She laughed and rolled her eyes. "Those shouldn't be questions that you need to ask. If someone says don't get into it, you don't get into it."

"I've got to weigh my options. That was an amazing cake."

"Then I'll tell you that I made marble cupcakes with peanut butter frosting." She pointed at her nose. "And spice cupcakes with caramel frosting. I still have the frosting bowls. Which do you want to sample?"

"I'll try the caramel first." He dipped his finger in the bowl. Putting it into his mouth, he slowly licked it off. "Now that's good. I do love peanut butter, though." She took the bowl he'd sampled from and put it into the sink to start washing up. After she'd turned the water on the bowls, she turned back to Mark and found him right beside her, dipping his finger into the peanut butter frosting bowl. When he turned toward her, only a few inches separated them. When he sighed, she could feel his breath on her face. As she was about to step back, he leaned forward, and his lips touched hers.

She took a half step closer. He reached his hand around the back of her neck and pulled her forward to deepen the kiss. He tasted of peanut butter. She slid her hands around his waist. She was home. Being in Mark's arms was like nowhere else. He was hers, and she was his, and it felt like he had finally realized that too, in the way that two people who belong together feel like one. She leaned forward, but he jumped back.

"Maddie. I am so sorry. I never meant for that to happen." He held up both hands. "Please forgive me. We have to keep this on a professional level, or I can't stay here." The stricken expression on his face was about as far as possible from the joy she'd felt.

She struggled to smile. "I understand." Even though she really didn't deep in her heart. "We were just close together, and we had a relationship a long time ago."

He nodded vigorously. The contractor who always seemed in control was no longer here. "Exactly. It was the frosting."

That put a smile on her face that felt more genuine. No one had ever accused her of using frosting as bait.

"Can you please forgive me?"

"There's nothing to forgive, Mark." And there wasn't. He took a step back and then another step back, bumping into one of the chairs at the kitchen table. He reached behind him to feel what it was and held onto it, seeming to need to steady himself.

"Don't worry about it, Mark. We're both adults now."

At that, his expression became more shuttered.

～

Maddie had reminded him of the past by mentioning the present. She wasn't the girl that he'd grown up with. She wasn't the Maddie he had loved with all his young heart. More than that, she was the girl who had broken his heart in such a way that it felt like it could never fully heal. He knew that didn't make sense to anyone but him.

But how could he get out of this situation without keeping the door open for it to happen in the future?

He cleared his throat. "I should have asked her when we met. Could you give me Lydia's phone number so I can send her a message and see if she'd be interested in dinner one night?"

Maddie turned toward the sink and started washing out the pans. "I'll text you her information when I'm done here. See you in the morning, Mark."

As he walked away, he marveled at his own stupidity. Lydia was the last kind of woman he'd be interested in dating. He never dated women who were flashy or bold. Then he remembered why he'd gone into the kitchen in the first place.

Sighing, he turned around and walked back to it, standing in the doorway. "Maddie, Noah is going to share the bed with Andy tonight. Andy's got a queen size, so there's plenty of room for them. No one will be sleeping downstairs."

She acknowledged him with a wave and continued her cleaning.

Mark went upstairs and brushed his teeth. Stretched out on his bed with his hands behind his head a few minutes later, he pondered the situation. He had kissed his former girlfriend, and she'd certainly kissed him back. He didn't know what to make of that. But he knew that he could not trust her. For just a moment, he stepped back into his teenage years. He could see Maddie at the airport in Juneau when he left to join the military. She'd been all smiles as she tried to be strong about the fact that he'd be gone for months in boot camp and training and could be shipped overseas any second after that. She said she would wait for him. Forever if that's what it took. That they belonged together. But she hadn't meant it.

When his doorknob turned, his heart leaped. Was she coming to see him? He partly hoped not because that would not be the Maddie he knew if she came to see a man in his bedroom at night. But he *would* like to talk to her.

Andy walked in instead. He came over and sat down in a straight-backed chair that looked to be an antique. "Okay, bro, what's going on? Tell me what's happening."

Mark vacillated between telling the truth and stonewalling him. The problem with brothers, or maybe it was a strength, was that they could read you sometimes better than you could read yourself.

"Don't even think of telling me 'nothing.'" Andy snorted. "I might have accepted that when you first came back to Alaska, but I've spent enough time with you here to get to know you again. What's going on, Mark?" With those words, he leaned back in his chair, folded his arms, and stared at his brother. "I've got all night."

Great. Andy, the logical computer nerd, had gone all touchy-feely on him and become Dr. Freud. "It's Maddie."

"And?" His brother drew the word out to the length of a sentence.

"And . . ." He hesitated for a moment. "I kissed her."

Andy grinned and slapped his thigh. "Maddie's back in our group? You're dating?"

He considered that for a second and firmly set that

thought to the side. "We are not. I made a mistake, and the past crept up on me. She was baking, Andy. You know how much I love cake and frosting and all things sweet."

His brother watched him carefully. "I do. But I've never noticed any romantic tendencies with you when you're around someone who is baking."

An incident from last week popped into his mind. "Have you heard that Mom tried to fix me up with someone a few days before I came here to start this job?"

Andy grinned. "Mom's matchmaking attempts are legendary for not only their frequency but for their lack of finesse and inaccuracy. She's never set one of us up and had it be someone we would be interested in."

Mark pointed to his left, to the room Andy shared with Noah. "She did well with Noah and Rachel."

"That was an accident. She was just playing a prank on him and didn't think they'd spend more than a half hour together."

"True. Well, this woman likes to bake. Mom invited her over to our house to work on some baking for a church event. A worthy endeavor, I might add. But then Mom realized she needed an ingredient from the store. And left me, quite conveniently, the only other person who was at home, to help the woman with that baking."

Andy grinned.

"I'm sure she's a lovely woman. But she was about ten years younger than I am. She talked incessantly and mostly about people I didn't know. When it wasn't that, it was baking technique. And you know, I don't care how you make it, I just enjoy eating it. I get excited about construction, but I don't think most people want to know all of the steps that go into installing a kitchen in their home. They just want to walk into it and make dinner in a beautiful place." Mark rubbed his temples. "I left as soon as Mom got home. I whispered 'nice try,' in her ear as I went by."

Andy's gaze narrowed. "What does that have to do with what happened tonight?"

What *did* it have to do with tonight? And then he realized something. "The thing is that when I walked away from that woman, I was happy. I'm happy being single. I need to do Maddie's job and then step away."

Andy stood. "If that's what you want to believe." He stared at Mark for just a moment and then left the room.

What did that mean? Before he turned off his light, he checked his email. As he went down the list, he found one with the subject line: *searching for home contractor.* He clicked on it. Stewart, a former high school friend, now lived in the Seldovia, Alaska, area. He'd heard that Mark had become a contractor and wanted to build a house. The attached plans showed that it was over four thousand square feet, so the project would take a while. Stewart had also included photos of the view of Kachemak Bay from where his house would sit, probably to show him he'd have a beautiful workplace. Mark replied to thank him for the offer, but that he was in the middle of a job.

Mark turned off his bedside lamp and closed his eyes. In the military, he'd developed the ability to sleep at almost any time or place. That didn't happen tonight. Visions of cupcakes danced in his head. Unfortunately, Maddie was frosting them and setting them down. He could see a trail in front of him with a chocolate cupcake every few feet. In the distance, Maddie set down another cupcake, took a few steps, and then another as though she was luring him closer to the baked goods. What a crazy image that was.

He fought the desire to reach down and pick up the cupcake closest to him. But when he looked forward, the cupcakes faded away as he watched her. All he saw was Maddie.

~

Madeline got up an hour early to slice the roast beef, hoping that a brother or two would be available to help her. When it came time to make the sandwiches, she pushed up her sleeves and soon had the thinnest slices of roast beef she could manage without a special slicing tool.

She heard movement upstairs and could hear water running, so someone was in the shower. Soon after, Andy came into the kitchen. He stopped and watched her for a moment. That seemed to be an O'Connell men's trait. Evaluate the situation before moving forward.

"Since I know that is for my lunch, and I, of course, want to make sure you have plenty of time to do it properly—" He grinned. Andy had always been the one to make her laugh. Not that Mark didn't, but Andy just seemed to smile a lot. He continued. "I think I should make sure that I have a hand in it, to be sure the boss gives me my share."

"I have a better offer. For those who help, I'll make a breakfast of bacon, eggs, and toast."

His grin widened. "I know for a fact that no O'Connell man would turn down that offer." He stepped over and washed his hands. Then she directed him on how to start the assembly line of sandwiches.

Noah walked into the room soon after. Both of the men were wearing button-down shirts and nice slacks for church. The water continued to run upstairs, and then it stopped.

Mark had clearly taken his shower, but would he join the group?

Andy explained the breakfast deal, and Noah enthusiastically took his place at the end of the line and began putting the sandwiches in plastic zipper bags. As minutes passed and the sandwiches continued to roll off the assembly line, Noah asked, "Um, Maddie, how many people do you think are at this job site?"

"I think there are a bunch of men working hard outside who eat like ravenous vultures."

He chuckled. "You may be right about that."

When she began stowing the completed sandwiches in a section of the fridge she'd cleared out, he asked, "Are you planning to come back after church to get them?" At her nod, he asked, "Will you need help with that? I want to make sure I get in the good graces of someone who's willing to make me breakfast."

She laughed. "I'd love the help." Still smiling, she carried over the last of the sandwiches and tucked them into the fridge. Then she pulled out what she needed to make the promised breakfast. As she cracked eggs into a large skillet, she heard footsteps on the stairs and then someone walking on the wood floors of the living room. Mark was drawing nearer to the kitchen.

She didn't look in that direction, but she did notice that Andy glanced from her to the doorway and then back again. Mark must have told him what happened last night. Heat rose in her cheeks. She wasn't even sure she would tell her sister about it. Ever. It was so embarrassing to realize that she was an easy pushover for Mark O'Connell.

She saw Noah give his brother a playful punch on his arm as Mark came in. "Are you going to help with breakfast?"

"I think I'll let Maddie take care of breakfast. I'm going to review some specs for her house on my computer." Mark gestured with his head toward the living room and vanished from sight.

Andy gave a frustrated sigh, reaffirming that he knew about the night before and was hoping his brother would change his mind. She would have said something to him, asked him to not bother or stop his efforts, but Noah was standing there. The more they could keep this contained the better. Instead of moving Jemma's projects and papers off of the dining room table, she asked Noah to set the small kitchen table, and they were soon crowded around it.

"Mark, if you don't come and get this, I'm going to eat your portion along with mine!" Noah yelled.

Mark hurried into the kitchen. Pulling out his chair, he said, "Don't even think about it, Noah."

Silence reigned as the men wolfed down their breakfasts. Then Noah said, "Maddie, when did you get to be such a great cook? I don't remember you caring about it when we were kids."

She spread some blueberry jam she'd found in the fridge on her toast. She knew that everything in there would be fresh because Jemma had told her that her doctor-sister went through their fridges when she visited to check for food safety.

"I learned to cook so that I could eat food I wanted to eat. At least that was the reason at first. When I decided I wanted to have a house and not have debt, I also decided that I had to save every penny. That meant that I didn't get to eat out very often, but I enjoy food. I had to become a much better cook. And the many cooking videos, TV shows, and blogs I had to choose from made it fun and easy."

Noah scooted back from the table and stood. "You can cook for me anytime. In fact, I think that Rachel would love it if you could teach her to cook. Mom might be a little more intimidating as a teacher, but you are about the same age as Rachel."

"That conversation could go really well or really badly."

Noah picked up his plate and headed for the sink with it. That's one thing she remembered about the O'Connell brothers—they had been trained to clean up after themselves. With five rambunctious boys, their mother had been smart to institute that from an early age.

Noah kept talking, love showing in his voice. "Rachel is an excellent businesswoman, and she's told me she wants to learn to cook. I think you have a lot in common, actually, because she also went to graduate school to get an MBA while she was working."

So tales of her life had already spread through the family. She knew she'd never had a conversation with Noah about that or talked about it while he was nearby.

"But she was very busy and living in a big city, so it was easy for her to go out and eat. From everything I've heard from her, it sounds like she put in a lot of twelve-hour days, sometimes more than that during the holidays."

Madeline knew very little about Noah's fiancée. "Will she be coming out to the job site? I'd like to meet her."

"I doubt she'll have time. She's working as fast as she can to get her clothing store open in Anchorage before the tourist season ends. She wants to capture some of that business." He used air quotes around *capture*. "She does business-speak a lot. I'm starting to understand what it means. And she's picked up a little bit about airplanes."

When they had all finished, Mark said, "While you're getting ready for church, Maddie, we'll clean up down here."

She didn't have to be told twice. That had never been her favorite task. It was just something you had to do when you finished cooking. And she'd been fortunate to have a dishwasher in almost every place she'd lived.

Upstairs, she changed into a summer dress and matching low heels. Her car could hold all of them, barely. It would feel tight with three men in it, but Andy had suggested it when they'd stepped out of the house together.

When he slid into the back with Noah, she knew he was matchmaking, but didn't know how to stop him. When he started to direct them to all slide into the same pew at church together with her first and Mark next, she decided she had to call a halt to this. She stepped back and motioned them on. "I'm going to run to the restroom before the service." No man would argue with a woman who had uttered those words.

She found Noah at the end of the pew when she returned. She sat beside him through the service and then drove the men home. Since they had all gone together—thank you, Andy—they all helped her load up the car.

The day at the worksite went well. Mark said he rarely worked on Sundays, but when he considered it family time. About an hour after they arrived, she served lunch so that it didn't stay in the car too long on a sunny day in the mid-sixties. They sat around on whatever they could find, several of them on the front steps, others on tree stumps, even the large rock off to the side of her front yard. As they were eating, Mr. and Mrs. O'Connell drove up in their motor home. Everyone stepped over to the side, and they pulled up into what had become their parking space.

Mrs. O'Connell hopped out with a smile on her face. "That was one of the most beautiful drives that I have ever been on. Have any of you ever driven the highway from Paxson to Mount McKinley? It's the Denali Highway, and it is gorgeous up there."

Mr. O'Connell stepped out. "She's right. It's a road through the middle of nowhere, though."

From the spot that he had commandeered on the front step, Noah said, "I have flown over it many times. It is pretty country. But the road doesn't look great from the air."

His mother shuddered. "There were moments . . . but we took it very slowly because we didn't want to damage the RV in any way. It's hard to believe that was the road to get to Mount McKinley National Park, now Denali, before the Parks highway went from this area straight up there."

"That's where I heard it. Did you go to the park?"

"No! Not in the summer. It's too full of tourists. We may give the drive another try in the fall. What do you think, Pop?" She turned toward her husband.

"I'd like to do that again. It is gorgeous. And the hills covered with low brush turning fall colors would make it even more beautiful."

Madeline watched the people around her. Most of them would have been her family if she'd married Mark. And those that weren't O'Connells were still family of family, all connected to one another in some way. Except her.

As her grandmother would say, she had made her bed, and now she had to lie in it. When the good-natured laughter ended. She passed out the cupcakes, and they were gobbled up down to the last crumb. She watched Andy eat one of each kind. When she glanced his direction with a questioning expression, he gave her a thumbs-up, and a grin lit his face. She did so love it when her food was enjoyed.

Mrs. O'Connell walked over to her. "It's coming along beautifully, isn't it?"

"It is."

"Mark's working out well as a contractor?"

"Well, considering that he's only the second contractor I've worked with and that the first one stole my money, ran off, and left me with barely a shell of a house, Mark's doing very well. He accounts for every penny he spends, probably just to keep me happy."

"No, dear. I think that's just who he is. The military, you know. He's very exacting."

She resisted glancing over at Mark, deciding to completely ignore him. She looked toward her house-to-be. "All of my dreams are coming true."

Mrs. O'Connell made a scoffing sound. "*All* of them?" Then she went over to talk to her husband and disappeared into the RV, leaving Maddie speechless.

What had she meant by that?

CHAPTER ELEVEN

*U*nfortunately, Sunday's victory morphed into Monday's trial. Madeline lay in bed that morning for longer than she should have. She could hear people moving around in the hall and decided to give them free rein before she got up.

When it grew quiet, she got out of bed, pulled on her robe, and peered out her door. No men in sight. She crossed the hall to the bathroom, showered, and got ready. She'd be spending the day with Mark O'Connell. A week ago, that might have been a challenge. After that kiss? More than a challenge!

She blew her hair dry and looked at her face in the mirror. "What happened to you, Madeline? You're mooning after a man just like you're back in high school. Of course, you were dating Mark then. Pull yourself together. You have been in meetings with the CEO of a multinational cargo company. You have flown halfway around the world for business. You survived fifty below zero weather on the North Slope when you had to investigate a cargo situation."

She squared her shoulders. "Madeline McGuire, you can do this."

She carefully did her makeup and hair so she'd know she looked her best, then went back to her room and changed into jeans and a T-shirt she knew matched her eyes. He might not want her, but she was worthy of having a man in her life, and she would look the part.

She found Mark alone in the kitchen.

"Everyone else is at the job site. I have a list of everything we need to look at and approve today to keep the build on track." He had a piece of paper in front of himself, and it had quite a list on it. She saw kitchen cupboards, bathroom counters, and much more.

Everything about Mark, from the way he sat to the way he spoke to the way he pushed the page over to her, said, *I am your contractor. We have a formal relationship.* Maybe today would be okay and easier than she'd expected.

"I'll grab a quick breakfast, and we can be on our way."

"You didn't happen to hold back any of those cupcakes, did you?"

Ah, there he was. Her Mark peeked out from behind the contractor he was playing this morning. "Well, I wasn't sure if Adam was going to show up at the house last night and feel like he'd missed out, so I did keep one of each cupcake." She bit her lip to keep from smiling. "You wouldn't want one of those, would you?" She kept an innocent expression on her face.

He laughed, and she loved the sound of it. "One of them?"

She took the two cupcakes out of a different cupboard than she'd used to hide them before—she knew she needed to keep these men guessing—and handed them to him. He greedily opened up the spice one and took a big bite. After he'd swallowed, he looked up at her. "You didn't want some of this, did you?"

She shook her head. "You don't have to share. Have fun. Are you always like this?"

He finished the first cupcake and started unwrapping the other one. "I don't usually have anything sweet in the house. Because I want to eat it all."

"I can see that." When he finished the cupcake, he went over to the sink to wash his hands. "I guess we'd better get going. We'll take my truck today because I think we'll be able to bring some of it back with us. I have a rental trailer reserved that we'll pick up on our way into town. I can bring home a lot of supplies with that."

For the most part, they drove in silence. But this silence was different from the one they'd had after taking Bree to the hospital. This time it felt strained. She needed to find a way to break that.

"Mark, are we still on track financially?"

His shoulders relaxed. He seemed grateful for a chance to talk about something neutral. "We are. I figured out a way to fit in that sliding glass door and deck that we talked about off the master. A lot is going to depend on what you choose for finishes. Whether or not you have expensive taste."

"I can assure you wholeheartedly that I have expensive taste."

Mark laughed.

"But I also know that I have a finite budget. Certain things are a must. I absolutely want granite countertops. A farmhouse sink would be wonderful if we can find a way to fit that in the budget. I know it costs more than a standard sink. And I want to have beautiful tile for the backsplash and in the bathrooms. I'm not sure if that means expensive?"

There was a question at the end of that last word. "It *can* mean expensive. Do you want to look at the tile first?"

Madeline thought about it. "The tile has to go with the countertops in both the kitchen and the bathrooms. Maybe we should choose the countertops first, or should we do it the other way?" She paused for just a minute. "I never thought about the overwhelming nature of all these decisions. Up until now, it's just been fun."

He reached out as though he was going to put his hand on hers to reassure her but pulled it back. "You will make a lot of decisions today. And by the end of the day, you might feel tired. But we'll get through it together." Before she could feel warm and fuzzy inside because he was going to be at her side, he added quickly, "I've done this with many clients."

He'd put her in her place, hadn't he? She was a client, and she would stay that way. She just needed to get that through her head. Or rather, her heart.

When Madeline walked into the tile store, it was such a beautiful sight that she could almost hear angels singing. Everywhere she looked there was tile. White, blue, brown, and black. Every color she could imagine.

The salesperson walked over to them, smiling politely.

Mark took control of the situation and greeted the man. "We're here to choose tile for a house that's under construction. Jemma Montgomery sent us."

Recognition crossed the man's face. "She has sent us many clients. We appreciate every one. What can I help you with today?"

Mark continued the conversation, which suited Madeline

just fine because her eyes were having a hard time finding one thing to focus on for more than two seconds. There was so much here!

"Kitchen backsplash, two full baths, and a powder room." Mark turned toward Madeline. "We haven't talked about this, but space-wise, it looks like we could fit a shower in your downstairs powder room, and the plumbing would be easy since it's on the ground floor. Would you ever use that office for a guest room or bedroom? As with the closet, having a full bathroom nearby could be helpful later if you sell."

There was that *sell* word again. She knew it was a good idea to keep the future in mind, but right now, all she wanted to focus on was enjoying her house. Still, it did make sense. "It's possible. And when my grandmother comes, the front steps alone will be a challenge. I'm not sure that I can ask her to climb the stairs to the second floor multiple times in the day. Let's do that."

The man jotted down the notes as they spoke. "Some clients prefer to look for tile for one room to begin with, and others want to browse and find what catches their eye and start with that, deciding later which room it would best suit."

Madeline pondered that. "I think I would like to walk through the store first. I'll do as you said and gather all of the tiles that I love. We can decide from there what to do." She turned toward Mark. "Does that work with what you have planned?"

He shrugged. "It's your show, Maddie."

She began weaving her way through the store, picking up a tile here and a tile there. For many of them, they'd made several-foot-wide squares of them to show what they looked like in a finished project. That helped. She had the wood beams on the ceiling in her great room, but she didn't want the house to be dark. And she didn't particularly like tan, so she ignored all of those tiles. She had soon amassed a collection of many tiles.

Mark had stayed behind, speaking with the salesperson. When he came over, he started laughing. "You have quite a nice selection there."

Madeline stared at the pile of tile and bit her lip. "I may have gone a little crazy."

Mark grinned. "A little?" When she looked up at him, feeling somewhat embarrassed by her zeal, he said, "Well, it's good that we have many tiles to select from when it comes to the design."

Their salesman had followed Mark over. "Nicely put. That is the way to a happy marriage."

They both turned toward him.

Mark said, "I'm her contractor."

She pointed at Mark and said, "He's my contractor."

The man smiled at them but had a confused expression. She hoped they looked like contractor and client, not more. Especially since their little exploration into more a couple days ago hadn't worked out very well.

Focus, Madeline. Focus.

She began sorting through the tile, putting them in stacks of where she thought they might work best. A pattern of shades of blue and white emerged, with some green mixed in.

The salesman stepped in. "Can you describe the style of your home?"

She answered without hesitating. "Rustic elegance."

The man seemed to mull that over. "So that means that you enjoy rustic textures like wood, but you also like to have a little bit of glamour thrown in? Am I hearing you correctly?"

"Perfectly. But I'm not someone who enjoys a lot of sparkles. More an understated bling."

"Your colors?"

"Teal, aqua, soft greens."

He sorted through the tile. "This would make a lovely kitchen backsplash then."

A tile that incorporated the blues and greens sat before her. This man knew what he was doing. She sighed. "It's perfect. What do you think, Mark?"

He watched with approval on his face. "I really thought you were going to choose something very girly. This is nice."

To the salesman, she said, "I'd like to have a cohesive color theme through my home."

He helped sort out all of the stacks, and they came up with a color scheme that included an aqua glass tile for a band around the master shower. The newly added down-stairs shower would be gray, so it would be neutral. And the bath upstairs, which would be shared by the other two bedrooms, was mostly white with a small decorative element of teal tile in an inset area for a shampoo shelf.

So now she had tile that she liked. But the question was whether she had stayed within budget or if she needed to start over on some of these. Mark had also helped guide her along the way, so she hoped they had done okay on price.

The salesman took the specifications and worked up the numbers. He came back with a figure. Mark had given her the number she had available to spend when they walked in, the number that she couldn't go over unless she was willing to shave the budget on other areas of the house, and they were under that. She let out a whoop and did a fist pump.

The salesman laughed. "I'm glad we got you exactly what you want. We can have all of this out to the job site tomorrow." He looked through everything they'd chosen. "Or would you like to take it with you today? I know we have everything in stock. We just need to have enough time to gather it together for you. You're a contractor, so I assume you have a truck."

Mark said, "I have a truck with a trailer outside."

The rest of the day went very well. The salesman pointed out white countertops with gray veining that looked similar to marble but were less expensive. She got the solid wood flooring she'd wanted from day one.

Everything they had chosen was either in the truck or due to be delivered the next day. Considering the distance between them and the rest of the country, she was grateful for the fact that she'd chosen in-stock items. After a quick lunch of burgers eaten in the car, they went to another store, ordered kitchen cabinets in a dark wood that would match her beams, and they were on their way home.

This time, the silence felt better. She was coming to realize that Mark only spoke when he had something to say. He didn't fill empty space with words. She both liked that and wondered if that would be a challenge if she was around him all the time. After they'd driven about ten minutes, she decided it could actually be pleasant because she could just sit quietly and watch the scenery go by on their way home. She never tired of the view of the mountains towering over them and the rushing rivers they crossed.

"I know you're taking the week off work, Maddie, but I'm not sure what to have you do on the job site. Drywall is going in on Thursday. Up until then, we're doing basic construction and nothing that someone who doesn't understand it can help with. I may start on siding with whoever is available."

Madeline looked down at her hands in her lap. She didn't want to be a nuisance. She just wanted to help. Her phone pinged with a text message, and she checked it. Her assistant was looking for some paperwork. She replied to the message and realized that she probably would be better off saving her leave for later. She sent another message saying that she would be at work the next day after all.

Her assistant replied, *I am glad. Today has been crazy.*

"I'll come to clean up the job site after work every day. But I've come to realize that I should just go to work and only take time off when I can help with painting and things like that. Things that are useful."

They took some turns off of the highway that weren't on her usual route home.

As she was about to ask Mark about it, he said, "We need to leave a lot of this somewhere safe. Jemma gave me directions to her storage area, which is massive because sometimes she has a lot of furniture that she is storing, but fortunately, right now is not one of those times. Andy's going to meet us there and help unload. I don't want to leave anything just sitting in a house with no doors and no windows. People in Alaska are basically good and kind—"

"But all it takes is one, right?"

"Let's just say that you have a tight budget. We don't want to have to purchase anything again."

Once they had done that, they went to the building site, where she donned her leather gloves and cleaned up. The dumpster had arrived, so she was able to throw much of the debris in there.

The entire time she cleaned, she kept an eye on Mark.

Oh, she did it unobtrusively, but she knew where he was all the time. It was kind of funny because she felt like she had gotten to know the man fairly well since he'd been here. And she liked him. She liked who he'd become. Something about him called to her. But she had to ignore it. At least she'd be at work for the rest of the week.

CHAPTER TWELVE

*W*hen she arrived at the job site on Friday, Madeline found a festive atmosphere. Mark's mother brought out sparkling apple cider in paper cups which she passed out to everyone. After a quick tour of the inside of the house, Madeline went outside, amazed at the progress.

Everyone gathered together in what would be a grassy front lawn, and Mrs. O'Connell raised her glass in a toast. "I don't know how you've all done it, but there is siding on the house, it has doors and windows and insulation, and all of the electric is wired. You installed drywall, and tomorrow the crew comes to tape it."

Maddie added, "I *think* I know what that means." She raised her cup. "Here's to all of your hard work." Everyone raised theirs and drank some of their cider.

Madeline wandered over to her house and peered through the open door of her house. And it did look like a house now. The door they'd bought on Monday was perfect, and the siding was up. Even though the home's exterior hadn't been painted yet, it would be gorgeous when it was done. She'd have to think about the color more to be sure, but a medium gray with white trim on the windows sounded beautiful to her.

When she got back over to the group, Adam said, "I think that our brother, the contractor, deserves a day off. What do the rest of you think?" He took a sip of his cider and watched. Something about his words seemed . . . off. Like there was a hidden meaning.

Mark just shrugged. "I don't know what I would do on a day off. Besides, I enjoy my work."

Without missing a beat, Adam said, "You need some time off. Don't you enjoy hiking? I know you hiked a lot in Colorado."

Mrs. O'Connell said, "Maddie, you've lived in this area for quite a while now, haven't you?"

Madeline gave a slow nod, concerned about where this conversation was going, and wondering if she could get control of it.

"I remember you hiking when you were growing up. Do you still enjoy it?"

She nodded again.

Adam said, "Then it's set. Maddie has wanted to help with her home's construction, and the contractor needs a day off. Her contribution can be to take him on her favorite hike."

Mark jerked his head around to stare at her.

She shrugged helplessly. She didn't think there was anything either of them could do to avoid this. Everyone else was watching them to see what would happen. They'd been ambushed.

When neither argued about the hike, everyone else wandered off, leaving Mark and Maddie alone. Or maybe that was part of the pre-decided plan. She took the few steps needed to be near him.

Mark said, "You know we've been set up, don't you?"

"It's kind of sweet, really. They love you, and they want you to be happy. They just don't realize that your happy is not with me."

He looked into her eyes in a way that made Madeline remember their kiss. She looked away. *Hide your emotions, Madeline.*

"We can go to a nearby trail for a short hike to make everyone happy." A destination came to mind.

Mark spoke before she could make the suggestion. "I don't need to run away from you, Maddie. But Adam is right. I seriously need a day off. And there's something about being in nature that soothes me. It makes me feel whole again. That's why I lived in a cabin in the woods in Colorado. I moved here, and not long after that, I started this job. I haven't had time to stop and reflect on much of anything."

She assumed their past and present would be considered in this reflection time. But she wouldn't hold out a whole lot of hope that in his reflection, he would decide that he wanted her in his life. "Well, if you want a genuine hike, one that is absolutely beautiful, I have just the place. It's nearby in the old gold mining area of Hatcher Pass. The beginning of the trail was a mining road and follows the creek. We'd pass old buildings and a waterfall. At the end, there's a great view."

"Now you're talking my language."

When Madeline looked up, she saw his mother watching them with a satisfied smile. Mrs. O'Connell thought she'd managed to fix her son up, but she hadn't done anything of the sort. Mark made that clear a moment later when he added, "I'd like to try to think of you as a friend, will that be okay? I know how to deal with friends."

It was better than enemies, better than anything she'd hoped for, so why not? "Sure. We're friends."

The next morning, Mark pulled his lunch supplies out of the fridge. "Do you want a sandwich?" He held up a pack of roast turkey. It hadn't taken him long to notice Maddie's frugal ways, and he wanted to help. "I have everything we need for lunch."

She grinned. "I know you have chips and drinks because I bought them for you."

As much as he tried to fight it—fight any attraction to her —he couldn't deny the fact that she made him smile.

He made hearty sandwiches and put them in plastic bags next to the bags of chips, apples, and drinks Maddie had piled up. "Do you have something to carry all of this in? Most of my outdoor activity gear is behind lock and key at a storage area in Kenai." He realized that included his hiking boots. Sneakers would have to do.

She put everything into her small daypack. Once they got going, Maddie's excitement about the trip became contagious. Her directions led them out of the broad valley that made up the Palmer area and to the Palmer-Fishhook Road. This gradually led them upward into the mountain pass with the Little Susitna River running beside the road. A hairpin turn was followed by another sharp bend in the road, this one leading to the Independence Mine State Historical Park. He slowed down.

"Keep going. But the old mine would be a fun outing for

another time. You can even bring a shovel and gold pan to try your hand at panning for gold."

He'd almost finished Maddie's house. There wouldn't be any more outings before he moved on, so that wouldn't be happening.

"This section of the road is high enough that snow keeps it closed more than half the year."

"I'm glad it's July because I'm enjoying it."

The road straightened out after a series of switchbacks.

"Slow down. We're almost to our turn." Madeline kept her eyes on the right side of the truck. "There!" She pointed to a small road. "Do we drive in a few miles and park there for the start of our hike, or park here and walk the whole trail?"

Mark eased his truck forward onto the dirt road. "Let's see what it's like. I could back out a short distance if the ruts become too deep." A blue sky with a few clouds skittering by lay overhead making it a gorgeous day. Bushes and branches hung next to the narrow dirt and rock road and occasionally scraped against his truck. The bad road grew worse. "I wouldn't hesitate to call this the worst road I've ever driven on."

He kept his eyes focused forward, but, from the corner of his eye could see her silently watching him. He wasn't sure if the drive had rendered her speechless or if she knew he had a punch line coming.

He added, "That would mean it was actually a road."

Maddie grinned. "The questionable news is that we have to make the return drive. Or you do. I'm considering walking and meeting you back at the main road." After a short pause, she added, "Just kidding. I wouldn't want to deprive you of my charm and wit."

"That's kind of you." He spun the wheel to miss a massive rock. His truck lurched to the left and slid, but he kept it under control as Maddie made a sound between a yelp and a groan.

"I'd have all this fun alone."

Maddie gripped the sides of her seat when they hit another large bump. "Besides, it is kind of fun. I don't know why humans enjoy driving over giant rocks and through pits for fun, but don't want to make it their daily drive. But we do."

When he parked the truck off the road, she released her grip, then opened and closed her hands, which must have lost circulation. "This area used to have a lot of mines. Even this old log cabin you parked next to with its rusted out roof must have been someone's home." She stepped out of the truck and opened the door to the back seat. "I'll get the lunches. We only have to walk a mile or so to get to Dogsled Pass. The view of a small lake in the brush is beautiful."

"Just being out here has released most of my stress." When Maddie caught his attention as she pulled out a map, he remembered that his hiking companion was the source of much of his stress. He inhaled deeply of the fresh air and let it out slowly. "I see wildflowers in green fields. It's beautiful here."

When they reached Dogsled Pass, he turned in a circle. "Thank you for this hike."

"Hiking has been my inexpensive way to have a mini vacation while I saved for my house. This is a favorite spot."

He continued to admire the view. "It's good to be back in Alaska."

"Why didn't you return here after you got out of the military?" She gasped and put her hand over her mouth. Then she said, "I'm sorry that was intrusive. You're my contractor."

For a moment, he slid his hand into hers and squeezed it, just like he did when they were dating. Then he dropped it and stepped away. "No, remember we agreed last night to be friends. Friends can ask questions. I felt like I needed space so I could become my own person. You may have noticed that my family has a way of being in your personal business all the time."

She chuckled. "As evidenced by the fact that you and I are on a hike today."

"Exactly. I wanted to build my own life. My mother makes it sound like I was a hermit. I was anything but. I have friends in Colorado. I lived in a small home in the woods. That was all I needed. She makes me sound like some sort of a mountain man in a cabin, but I had hot and cold running water."

Maddie grinned. It felt so good to spend this time with him. "I thought maybe something happened in the military, something that had left you with emotional challenges, for lack of a better way to express it."

He ran his hand over his face. "I have friends with those struggles, but I was fortunate. I was never shot at, was never on the front lines. Yes, I was deployed to other countries, but was never in true danger."

"Why did you leave the military? Why didn't you just stay in if it was going well?"

He turned and started walking and motioned for her to continue with him. "I know we talked about my being career military, but I eventually felt like I needed to do something different with my life." They retraced their steps back to his truck.

As they climbed back into the vehicle, Madeline asked, "I have a goal of walking Resurrection Pass some time. Would you be up for that?"

They began the slow drive back to the main road. "We can go whenever you want. Or is there something I'm missing?"

"It's thirty-nine miles of wilderness and is hiked over multiple days."

He focused on picking his way through a rocky section before replying. "That sounds perfect. I need to get established here this summer, at least what's left of the season. That's one thing I will miss about Colorado. Summer lasted longer there, even in the Rockies, than it does here."

She laughed. "The weather here has been changing in recent years. You may be surprised at what you will find at a time when there was always snow in the past."

When they finally made it to the road, they drove back toward Jemma's house with their conversation centered again on their safe topic, people they used to know.

CHAPTER THIRTEEN

The past was not just the past.

Mark watched Maddie go upstairs to bed.

They'd been alone in the kitchen when he kissed her, and they'd been alone on the hike when he'd held her hand. He'd always loved holding her hand. When he'd been a teenager and shyly reached for it, he'd wondered if she'd want him to do that, but she'd gently squeezed it, and his heart had felt full.

But the touching and kissing had to stop. For his sake.

It hurt too much every time he touched her, every time that emotion, his old love for Maddie, started to creep out. Allowing that love to rekindle would give her the power to hurt him again. He'd trusted her in the past, and that hadn't gone well. He still didn't know why she'd broken up with him. He leaned back on the sofa and tapped his fingers on his thighs.

He had loved the eighteen-year-old Maddie with all of his heart. He'd planned a future with her. He would never make that mistake again. He needed to make sure that they were never alone. Never. Inch by inch, he felt closer to her each time they were alone together. She amazed him, she intrigued him, she made him laugh and smile as he hadn't done in years. But she also brought up an ache in his heart that he had not felt in years. He may not be able to walk away from the job—because he would never do that to her or any other client—but he could certainly make sure that they were never alone together.

He picked up his phone and sent a text message to all four of his brothers.

Need a brothers meeting for ideas about Maddie.

He wanted to get them together and explain what he needed from them. Jack hadn't been here on the job site yet, but he included him because he needed every one of his brothers' input. The only time they could get together with the certain knowledge that Maddie wouldn't be there was during the day on weekdays.

Maybe one of them would have another suggestion on how to fix this. Scratch that. This wasn't fixable. He needed to get through this situation and walk away without any more pain.

One by one, his brothers texted back. Andy had stayed on longer since Jack's work had kept away longer than he'd expected. Adam was almost always available in the summer, so any time should work for him. Noah had early flights the next morning but said he could be there mid-afternoon. Jack said he'd been wrapping up a project and would leave early in the morning.

Mark sent a message: *Meeting at 3.30 p.m. at the job site tomorrow.*

Progress on the house continued at a rapid pace. The wood flooring had been brought inside and left to adjust to the humidity. Now his team members could install it. Once it was installed, sanded, stained, and sealed, they could finish the rest of the house. This was the home stretch.

He was glad that Jack would be here soon. They'd assigned him the task of tiling. He'd always been the most careful with jobs like that when they were growing up. It hadn't been a surprise when he'd first become a jeweler and then a photographer because he was both artistic and good with technology, something both professions needed. He'd always been the chosen one when it came to patience, too, a trait that might help when tiling.

Now that the stairs were in, they had a place to sit and talk. By 3:15 p.m., everyone had arrived and were seated around him on the stairs.

Mark said the words he'd practiced. "I need for you to be a buffer between Maddie and me."

Andy's brow furrowed. "A buffer? Has she done something wrong?"

Mark rubbed the back of his neck. Every time he thought about this, his muscles tensed up.

Before he could form a reply, Noah stepped in. "If I understand this correctly—and please correct me if I'm not —Maddie's presence is a strain on you. We're guys and we don't talk about emotions very often, but we all know that she hurt you when she broke it off when you joined the military."

All of the brothers nodded in agreement.

"It was ugly. I was glad she left town before you came back for your first furlough," Andy agreed.

Relief surged through Mark. His brothers understood him.

Adam, always the brother who kept things organized, said, "Exactly what do you have in mind, Mark?"

"I thought I could be friends with Maddie, but I can't. I want you to make sure that I am never alone with her."

Silence fell over the group. He was sure that this group had never been silent before.

Andy spoke up. "Okay. Are you sure that you want that? It feels a little high school to me."

Great, now one of my younger *brothers thinks I'm being immature.* "Let's try to have everyone act subtle."

Andy laughed. "I know this is not a laughing matter, and I'm sorry, Mark, but I think that one of us running over to you every time she comes near you is going to be anything but subtle."

When Mark pictured that happening, he realized that his brother was right. He just didn't have another solution. "No matter how right you are, this is what I want."

"So we need to be subtle, but get to your side as quickly as we can? I just want to make sure that I understand." Noah had a note of sarcasm in his voice.

This could be a bad idea. "Maybe—"

Just then, their mother walked through the front door. When she saw her boys clustered together, she walked toward them with a puzzled expression on her face. "Are you having a party that I wasn't invited to?"

Mark said in a low voice, "Just go with the plan for now."

A couple of them shrugged, but they all got up.

In a louder voice, he said, "Thank you for doing so well with the work. The house is coming along very nicely. I couldn't have done it without you."

His mother beamed at them. "It's so nice to see my boys working together."

Every word he'd said was true. He hadn't lied to her. But she did not need to know the rest of the situation. She'd pushed him and Maddie together for that hike, and that couldn't happen again. It just couldn't. He could still feel her hand in his.

He had always subscribed to the thought that real men didn't cry, and that had certainly been reinforced in the military. But every time he wanted more with Maddie but knew he couldn't have it, he came close to tears.

On the bright side, Maddie's house was almost done. Within a couple of weeks, they should be out of here. She would move in, and he would never see her again.

Why didn't that make him happy?

As she drove from work to the job site, Madeline realized that she'd soon have her house, and Mark would leave her life. That thought hurt. She put her hand on her chest. And friendship with Mark was such a challenge when her heart wanted so much more.

She probably needed to accept that he'd leave, but she knew there was an important thing she had never done, and she needed to before Mark left. She had never apologized to him, and that hung between them. They may not have a future together, but the least she could do was to mend the past.

Entering her driveway, she saw him over at his work table, going over some paperwork. Apologizing to him tonight would be her number one goal. Now she just had to get him alone.

Madeline started picking up the debris slowly, heading

toward Mark, who was alone. As she headed that direction, Andy came out of the house and walked up to Mark, arriving at his side seconds before she did. She turned away and continued with her task.

When she threw the last piece of debris into the dumpster, she noticed Mark walking into the house. As casually as she could, she pulled off her gloves and tucked them in her back pocket while walking in that direction. She found Mark in her kitchen area. This was her chance. But then Noah, who had been working with his father to install glass French doors off her downstairs office, all but *ran* over to the two of them. This was either a very strange coincidence, or Mark had told his brothers to never let her be alone with him.

Had it come to that?

Mark glanced over at her, ignoring the fact that his brother stood next to him. "Maddie, I hadn't thought about it before, but instead of the standard cabinets in this corner, we can actually install a pantry with a door on it and about six shelves inside. That would give you a lot more storage."

She'd always wanted an actual pantry. "I like your plan. But we've already bought the cabinets. Won't that be a waste?"

"We bought stock cabinets, and we can return what we don't use, so it may actually save us money. I haven't run all of the numbers yet. At the very least, it will not cost more."

"That sounds like just what I want. Thank you for thinking of it." She gave him her best smile.

"We'll get it done."

He and Noah walked away, Mark talking the whole time about some aspect of the building project.

That man! So much for her making an apology today. And what had happened to their newfound friendship?

She probably deserved the treatment she was getting, but that didn't make her like it any more. At what point was the past the past?

She'd like to have a future with Mark, and the only way for that to be possible was for him to forgive her. She needed to be the one to start that process. As she watched him walk away, though, she wondered for a second if the way he was treating her was any indication of the man he had become. She didn't feel cared for. He certainly hadn't been that way on their hike.

After that failure, she gave up on attempting to talk to Mark there. Maybe she could catch him alone in the kitchen at their temporary home. Without saying anything to any of them, she left and went home to come up with a plan. Maybe she could capitalize on Mark's sweet tooth.

She baked a cake so that smell would be what greeted him when he walked in the house. It would be in the kitchen, and she would be sitting there with her laptop.

When she started to feel a little bit pathetic, she decided that it wasn't that she was running after the man so much as needing to fix what had happened before. He needed to be able to heal, and so did she. Forgiveness would be the first step if he was able to manage that. She didn't blame him if he couldn't, but she hoped he could. And maybe they could still be friends. It was a good place to start.

A couple of hours later, the men came home. "Maddie's been baking!" She knew Noah's voice.

She looked up from her laptop and saw three men taking their coats off. At least he hadn't brought all of his brothers. The fewer there were, the more chance she had of talking to Mark alone.

Andy stood in the kitchen doorway. "It smells fabulous. Do we get some of whatever it is?"

She had to grin. Laughing, she said, "Yellow cake with chocolate frosting."

"We would definitely like some of that. Do we have any milk?"

She pointed to the fridge. "Somebody put it on the shopping list, and I picked it up tonight on the way home."

"Awesome." He called through the doorway. "Do you guys all want milk too?"

"I do," Noah answered.

Finally, Mark spoke. "Of course."

Andy cut slices of cake and put them on three plates, then he poured three glasses of milk. Noah walked in and helped carry the milk. But Mark never entered the kitchen.

She sat at the table, dumbfounded. But she wouldn't be knocked down. All she wanted to do was apologize to him. If he was going to play this game—which reminded her very much of being in high school—then two could play. As long as she was on the computer, she went ahead and sent an email to her supervisor and her assistant saying that she would be out tomorrow, that she was needed on the job site. This week at work hadn't had anything critical going on. She hoped tomorrow would be the same.

As Mark got ready for bed, he thought back over the evening. The keep-him-away-from Maddie situation bordered on ridiculous. Fortunately, his time near her would come to a close soon. He'd grown to enjoy the Palmer area, though, so maybe he should search for a place to live here.

He went to his room and closed the door. As much as he might enjoy that, he would be Maddie's nearby neighbor, and that wouldn't be a good plan.

No. Living within driving distance of his family was high on his list of priorities, but that couldn't be near Maddie. He sat on the edge of his bed and scrolled through his emails. The one he'd received from his high school friend, Stewart, stopped him. The job in Seldovia could help. There wasn't even a road connecting it to the rest of the world, so he wouldn't be as tempted to leave. He'd have to take a plane or boat to leave, but when he did his family wouldn't be far away.

He fired off an email to Stewart to ask if he still needed a contractor.

CHAPTER FOURTEEN

*M*adeline needed a sister to sister consultation. She called Sadie. "Busy?"

"Mmmph."

She was probably reading a textbook. "I decided to apologize to Mark, but it isn't working. His brothers are always around him."

"The apology is a long time coming, Madeline. I'm glad you're going to do that. It might heal the two of you."

"I hope so. When I first thought of it, that's what I wanted. So now I just need to do it. But the brothers!"

"They've always been close."

"No, you don't understand. I can't catch him alone because there's always one of them around, and if there isn't, one races over."

Silence greeted her, so she looked at her phone to make sure that her sister was still there. "Hello?"

"I'm here, Madeline. I'm just astounded. How are you going to talk to Mark alone if you can't *get* him alone?"

She stared up at the ceiling. "I need suggestions. That's why I called. Well, and to check up on you."

Her sister chuckled. "Is there any time that he *is* alone? Other than in the bathroom, because that's more than a little bit creepy."

"His job is to be the contractor on the site, and he often goes there before anyone else. His brothers usually join him a little bit later. That's it! I will be there when he arrives on the site. Thank you!"

"Madeline, wait! How are you going to do that? How much earlier are you going to have to get up to beat this man to the site?"

"I think about 4:30." She shuddered. "But it's worth it. Mark had said he wanted to be friends, but that doesn't seem possible. If we can't move forward with a relationship, I want this chapter of my life closed. The silly thing is that, for a moment, I thought we could have a future together again."

"Let me know how it works. I still have about ten days left here." They chatted about Maddie's niece and her sister's classes before hanging up. Then Madeline turned out the light and closed her eyes. She needed to get some sleep because morning was coming much earlier than it usually did.

Madeline quietly tiptoed across the hall to take a shower and get ready. She was happy to see that no one else was up when she left.

The question was, where should she put her car so that no one knew she was at the house site? She finally decided she'd park it beyond her house at the side of the road. Mark and whoever else came along to start the workday would pull into her driveway and not continue further on the road.

She walked through the woods onto the property. When she got to the door, she was glad that she had been given a key when they'd installed the door. It hadn't meant much at the time other than a major step in her home's construction. Now it was handy.

She relocked the door so no one could tell she was there. This was a long shot, and it would be hard to explain if someone other than Mark arrived first. But she'd noticed that he was always the first one out in the morning and the last one home.

The plan's one flaw was that he sometimes brought another of the guys with him. She hoped this wasn't one of those days.

Where could she hide while she waited for him? She'd heard the men talking last night, and the master bath had been mentioned. Mark said he needed to do something before the tiling could begin. She'd hide in her master closet. Feeling more than a little bit like a creepy stalker, she hurried up the stairs and into it, closing the closet door all but a crack before sitting down.

She heard sounds outside like a vehicle pulling up on the gravel drive. A door slammed, and then someone entered the house. What if it wasn't Mark? How would she get out of here without anyone knowing she'd been here? The thing about having stairs and a great room beyond them was that everybody could see you going up or down those stairs. She'd have to go out onto the new deck and find a tree to shimmy down so she could escape unseen.

But her wait was rewarded when Mark walked into the bedroom and headed straight for the master bath. Once he was in that room, she slowly opened the closet door and listened to see if she heard any other footsteps or voices. When she didn't, she made her way over to the bathroom door.

"Good morning, Mark."

He jumped and dropped the wrench he'd been holding. "I didn't realize you were up when I left the house."

"I got up early this morning. There is something I need to talk to you about."

He stood and looked like he was about to come up with an excuse for why he needed to leave when she held up her hand. "Mark, please. I need to apologize to you for what I did when we were teenagers."

His expression clouded. "You don't need to do that, Maddie."

"Yes, I do. First, I need you to understand what happened. It doesn't excuse anything, but I do need you to have the whole story. Maybe it will help you heal."

He nodded. "I'm listening." His tone had grown harsher, less like the man that she'd been spending time with lately. He also stood at attention. He'd gone into military mode. Well, that was okay as long as he was listening.

"I was eighteen, Mark. The man I loved with *all my heart* —" she emphasized those words, but his expression remained unchanged "—was going away, and he would not be back for a long time. I planned to go to college, but we talked about me not doing that and joining you. Remember?"

"I remember. That might not have been our best plan. You'd talked about going to college as long as I could remember."

"What you don't know is what happened after you left, but before college."

"After you promised to wait for me and that we would have a future together? Is that what you're referring to, Maddie?"

She would not let him stop her from saying what she needed to say. "My parents sat me down and talked to me. They said I was young, that I had my life in front of me, and I needed to go to college. What we had together was young love. It would pass."

She took a deep breath and continued. "Then my grand-mother flew into Juneau to talk to me. She said, and I quote, 'Madeline, you need to live the life that God intended for you to live. Go to college. Mark is going to be in the military for years. Long-distance relationships are painful and difficult and do not work.' All of my friends said essentially the same thing. I was a kid, Mark. I didn't have a whole lot of life experience. I had my parents, my grandmother, everyone I knew, saying that this would not work. I wrote you a letter, and I tried to make it as kind as I could."

He made an ugly sound. "Are you through?" At her nod, he continued. "You were surrounded by family and friends. I was alone in a strange place, and I was scared. Do you know what they do in boot camp? It isn't just in the movies where they shoot over you to strengthen you for the future. Bullets flew over my head. I was eighteen. But I was surviving it. I felt like the conquering hero because I had my girl back home. We'd talked about a future together, about marriage and children. We were all but engaged."

Mark pointed at her. "And then I got that letter from you. Do you know what that did to me? How it hurt my heart?" He tapped his chest. "For days, I could barely even function. Finally, my CO talked to me and said that if I didn't shape up,

I was going home. I could not bear that humiliation. I'd joined the Army, and I intended to succeed."

She had never heard anger like this from Mark. She could see the boy he'd been in the man that he was now and how much she'd hurt him. "Mark, I'm sorry. I'm sorry. I'm sorry." The tears that had started while he was shouting fell down her cheeks. "I hoped that maybe we could have a future together. I've enjoyed being with you again."

"The future? You shattered my trust, Madeline. I have not wanted a relationship beyond anything casual since then."

"Don't you feel anything for me?" She swiped at the tears across her cheek and swallowed a sob.

An expression she'd almost call love came over his face as he stared at her. Then it vanished and was replaced by more anger and what she would describe as loathing. "Madeline McGuire, I thought I might be able to, but you shattered my trust, and even an apology hasn't helped mend that. Your house will be finished in about two weeks. I'm going to take a job in Seldovia after that, so I'll leave the day it's done and be far away from here and you."

Madeline felt like she had been slapped. She turned and ran from the room and down the stairs, the tears intensifying with every step. She dashed tears off her cheeks with her hands and somehow made it through the great room without tripping.

She paused at the front door to wipe away the tears in case someone else had arrived. Then she raced down the front steps. Her foot caught on something, and she tumbled forward, putting her arms up over her face to protect it.

The world went black as pain crashed through her.

CHAPTER FIFTEEN

*M*addie had screamed. Was she that upset? Mark almost ignored it and kept working, but he couldn't quite make himself do that. Stepping out of the room and going to the head of the stairs, he saw the front door standing wide open. It needed to be closed to keep everything dry and protected. Surely Maddie knew that?

But when he went down to close it, he saw her lying on the ground at the bottom of the front steps.

"Maddie!" He ran down the steps and around the toolbox he'd left there. When he reached out to touch her, he realized that she wasn't moving, and her body was lying in an unnatural position. "No!" He put his fingers against her neck to check her pulse. Her heartbeat reassured him that she was alive. Brushing her hair off her cheek, he said, "Maddie? Can you hear me?"

She didn't stir. He stood and took his cell phone out of his pocket. Hitting 9-1-1, he explained the situation to the operator and soon heard sirens in the distance, then growing louder as the ambulance drew closer and finally pulled up her drive.

A man and woman jumped out of the vehicle when it stopped and raced to her side. He stood off to the side, feeling helpless. After they conferred with each other, the man stood and made a call.

Mark went over to the woman. "She's going to be okay, isn't she?" He knew that was the standard question, but it had to be asked.

The woman looked up at him with an expression that he never wanted to see again. "We're calling for a helicopter. We think she'd be better off at one of the larger hospitals in Anchorage."

With the call completed, the man returned. "They're on the way. Dispatch is sending us to a field not far from here where a helicopter can land."

Mark watched as they carefully lifted Maddie's body onto a gurney. She must be in tremendous pain, but being unconscious, her expression remained unchanged, and she didn't flinch. They loaded her into the ambulance, and the woman climbed into the back with Maddie.

Mark hurried over. "I'm going with her."

"Are you a relative?"

The biggest lie of his life came out of his mouth. "I'm her fiancé."

The woman gave a pointed glance at Maddie's left hand, which was missing a ring, but instead of arguing, she waved him in and closed the door. The driver turned around and drove down the driveway to the road, turning right.

As they crested a hill, through the back windows Mark saw Maddie's car parked beside the road. Mystery solved.

That's how she'd gotten to the house. She had planned this very carefully.

And he had lashed out at her in anger. And now she might be dying.

The helicopter was waiting in an open field with its blades turning. They transferred the gurney from the ambulance to the helicopter. He found a seat inside and rested his head in his hands. What had he done?

He sent a group text to his brothers, his parents, and Jemma.

Maddie fell at the job site. I'm on an emergency flight to Anchorage with her.

Replies came in, asking questions, questions he didn't have answers to. So he responded to the whole group:

She's unconscious and I think she has broken bones. Will update when I know more.

His phone vibrated again with replies including, "Oh no!" and "We're on our way!"

At the hospital, Mark waited in the helicopter while they unloaded Maddie. Then he hopped down and followed closely behind. Inside, he was directed to a waiting area. She would first be undergoing tests so the doctors could determine how badly she'd been injured. He settled in for a long wait.

About a half-hour later, Jemma texted that she had arrived, and then his brothers started arriving. He gave them directions to his location. Before long, he was surrounded by family and Maddie's friends. Jemma must have also told her sisters because Bree arrived with her baby.

"Explain what happened, please, Mark," Jemma asked.

Did he tell them what he'd done, or did he just say she'd tripped and fallen?

He might as well own up to everything. None of this would have happened if he'd been kinder.

Folding his arms, he leaned back, prepared for any backlash. "All of you know that Maddie and I dated in high school, and we planned to have a future together. You probably also know that Maddie sent me a letter when I was in the military and broke up with me." He took a deep breath before continuing and let it out. "She came to the site early today to apologize to me, to explain what had happened and why she had done it. I didn't take her apology well. I got angry."

Adam put his hand on Mark's arm. "You didn't hurt her, did you?"

Mark stared at him. "Do you really think that I could ever hurt a woman?"

"I'm sorry. I shouldn't have even thought that for a second, and I certainly shouldn't have spoken those words."

"Then what happened?" Andy asked, bringing them back to the subject at hand.

"I made her cry. I thought I was the only one on-site this morning. I had set my toolbox on one of the steps, knowing that I would come back and use them before anyone else arrived. She'd parked her car up the hill and was waiting for me inside."

"She had planned this pretty carefully," Holly said.

They all watched him, waiting to hear what happened next.

"She ran out the front door after we spoke. All I can figure is that she raced down the steps, tripped over the toolbox, and flew through the air to hit the ground. I don't think she could have just tripped and fallen normally because she's unconscious, and her head doesn't seem to be bleeding. She must have hit the ground hard." Mark leaned forward with his head in his hands. "It's all my fault." Tears filled his eyes, and he swiped at them, so no one would see them.

Adam sat next to him. "You didn't mean to hurt her or anyone."

He knew that his brother's words were true, but he also knew that Maddie was here in this hospital because of his actions.

Mark couldn't help checking his watch every few minutes. Conversation stirred around him, but he sat silently. He didn't feel like talking.

Three hours had passed when his parents called from the parking lot. He told them where they were, and they ran in the door minutes later. His mother hurried over to him, and he stood to be enveloped in her hug. She made him feel better than he had all morning.

When he stepped back, she put a hand on each of his cheeks and looked into his eyes. "Our Maddie is going to be okay, right?"

Before he could go into another explanation of her accident, a doctor walked through the door into the waiting room, wearing a weary expression, but smiling. Mark hoped he had good news. When he saw the group, the doctor paused and asked, "Which one of you is the fiancé?"

All eyes turned toward Mark. He ignored them and said, "I am, sir."

The doctor walked over to him. "She should be fine. She did not hit her head. It looks like she used her arms to protect her face as she fell. Her arms are scraped up, her left arm and right ankle are broken."

Mark winced, and he heard a couple people say "ouch."

"As soon as the swelling is down, we'll put a cast on both.

We have set her arm, and it's in a splint. So is the ankle. We're waiting for her to regain consciousness."

Mark, his hand on his chest, stepped back. "She still hasn't woken up?"

The doctor shook his head. "We've done all of the usual tests, and the results are good. But she has not moved a muscle. I or someone else will keep you updated." He seemed to notice Bree for the first time. "Are you part of this family, Dr. Kincaid?"

"My sister married into the family, and I'm a friend."

"Good to see you and the baby." With that, he left.

Mark stood there for a moment, not knowing what to do. When the doctor was almost to the door, Mark called to him. "Can we see her?"

He turned around. "This is quite a group. Let's say two at a time. The fiancé can stay, though." When the doctor had left, everyone gathered around him.

His father said, "Is there something about your relationship that we don't know, son?"

Mark followed the doctor. "No, Dad. They weren't going to let me go with her, and I had just caused this accident. There was no way I was going to let my Maddie get on there alone." He stopped as he realized what he'd said. Eerie silence around him that quickly turned to a buzz of voices made him realize that everyone else had noticed it too.

He continued out the door and down the hallway. Every step brought him closer to the realization that he had never stopped loving Maddie. He'd buried it under anger and pain. That was why he'd never been able to love anyone else or to have a serious relationship with another woman.

After finding Maddie's room number, he stood outside her door. As he stepped into the room, keeping his eyes on

Maddie's silent, still form, he realized that she had never found anyone else either. Then he remembered what she'd said about wanting a future with him again.

She'd reached out to him, and he had pushed her away in the most brutal way he possibly could. He didn't deserve her love, but he was going to do everything he could to win her back. He pulled a chair over beside the bed, took her hand in his, and sat down. He'd stay here until Maddie woke up.

Sometime later, he woke up with his shoulders stiff and his right arm numb from being in the same position for so long. He rotated his shoulder and shifted in his seat.

When he looked over at Maddie, he found her staring wide-eyed at him. "How are you?"

She had a sweet smile as she said, "What a lovely dream. I know I'm dreaming because you're Mark, and you're being kind to me and holding my hand." She tried to move her left arm and looked down. "It's one of the dreams where you can't move." She sighed and clasped his hand tighter. "It's even better than a flying dream." She closed her eyes.

He slid his hand out of hers and rushed to the nurse's station to let them know that she had woken up.

Minutes later, a doctor came into the room and examined her further. "I think we can now say that she's going to be fine. It's good that you were here when she woke up. But I think you can get some rest now."

He wasn't even sure what time it was. He checked his watch and saw that it was just after 10:00 p.m.

The nurse added, "One of your brothers has been waiting for you. He said he'd take you home when you were ready."

"Are you sure she's going to be okay?" He looked down at Maddie.

When he looked up again at the nurse, she smiled. "As

sure as we can ever be about these things. She'll need you more tomorrow. We've given her something to make her sleep and for the pain. She probably won't be awake again all night."

She left, and he stood there, staring at Maddie for he didn't know how long. Then he went out and found Andy asleep in the waiting room.

He jostled his brother's shoulder. When Andy opened his eyes, his first words were, "Is she okay?"

Mark smiled, the first real smile he'd had in a while. "She woke up, and it looks like she'll be okay. But she's back asleep now. Let's go home." As they walked out, he added, "I'll be back in the morning."

Andy put some music on in the car as they drove in silence for a while.

When Mark was ready to talk, he went over everything that had happened between him and Maddie since they'd started her project. "I have been the biggest idiot on the planet. Maddie was in front of me, and I kept pushing her away."

Andy turned off the music. "I'm not in a relationship, so I'm not commenting from personal experience. But I can say that it looks like you made a mistake. But then again, it wasn't as though she'd expressed any interest in you, right? Women can be confusing creatures."

But was that it? Mark thought back over the last few weeks. Her words, her actions, the kiss, the way she'd tightened her fingers around his hand when she was holding it, they all added up to her showing interest.

"Although we've watched the two of you the last few weeks, and we all agreed that she liked you a whole lot more than you liked her."

"I think we just circled right back around to *I was the biggest idiot on the planet.*"

Andy gave him a light punch to his shoulder. "It's kind of hard to argue with logic like that."

As Mark got ready for bed, he thought about the different outcomes this day could have had. If she hadn't made it, the blame would have sat squarely on his shoulders. He shook it off. "She is going to be okay, and that's what matters." He'd be there for her as much as he could.

Mark was just as exhausted after his morning shower as before, even though the hot water normally woke him up. At the top of the stairs, he heard voices. Halfway down the stairs, he could see that his whole family filled the small living room. "Are you here to read me the riot act? I know that I was a jerk, and Maddie's lying in a hospital bed because of me."

His father stepped forward. "Mark, we all make mistakes. You've owned up to it, and that's what's important. Now we just have to do everything we can to take care of Maddie."

Adam said, "We've talked about it, and we figured out that we can finish this house in a week if we all work every day on it."

"But some of you have jobs. How can you do that?"

"We sorted all of that out. We'll be here for Maddie. Bree estimated that they'll keep her in the hospital for a week because she'd been unconscious for so long. She also has to heal enough that she can stand on one leg and get around."

As he considered what they needed to do to finish the house, he had to agree. "Okay, let's go over to the job site." He continued down the stairs, but no one moved. Stopping, he asked, "What else is going on here?"

His mother went into the kitchen and motioned for him to follow her. She pulled out a chair, gestured for him to sit there, then sat in the one next to him.

"Mark, we all heard you call her 'my Maddie' last night. Do you want her to be your Maddie?"

He felt tears pricking at his eyes. He would not cry again. "It's too late for that, Mom."

She put her hand on his arm. "Mark, it's never too late. We all noticed Maddie's behavior around you, how often she looked at you. The girl never stopped loving you. She just took bad advice when she was still too young to know the difference."

He felt a glimmer of hope. "What do I do, Mom? How do I show her that I want her in my life?"

His mother stood. "Court her. It's old-fashioned, but women like to know that they're special to someone."

"Mom, she's in a hospital bed, and she's immobilized because she has two broken limbs."

"That may work in your favor because you'll know exactly where she'll be for a while."

He laughed. "Only you could find the sunshine in that."

"It's my trademark. That and flowers." With those words, she exited the room, his last image of her a yellow shirt with flowers on it. He heard others leaving and finally left himself. When he got behind the wheel of his truck, he sat there for a minute.

He had two choices right now. Go to the job site and finish the job. That would show her he cared, wouldn't it? *Or* he could spend time with her in the hospital.

He decided on the hospital. Work could be done later.

Driving, Mark tested the words out loud. "I'm going to court her." They sounded odd to his ears. He stopped and picked up some flowers. Not just any flowers, though. He wanted flowers that were the colors she'd chosen for her house. He had a feeling those were the colors she most enjoyed.

Maddie was asleep when he walked into the room. The heart monitor showed she was okay, and everything was working well.

A nurse followed him in the door. "She's been sleeping. We woke her up a couple of times to make sure she was okay, but she was very groggy. I'm glad you're here."

Mark set a vase filled with blue flowers down on a small table off to the side. Then he sat beside Maddie and held her hand again. This time he'd come prepared with a book to read, so he tried to focus on that, but his thoughts kept wandering to what had happened yesterday. To the words he had said to this woman lying here in this bed.

Mark felt movement beside him and looked up.

Maddie's eyes were open, and she was scanning the room. They stopped on him, and she jerked back, wincing as she did so.

He set down his book. "Be still, Maddie."

She tried to raise her left arm and then stared at it. Then she lifted up her right hand and pointed at him. "You were here last night, too, weren't you? It wasn't a dream that you were nice to me." Tears welled up in her eyes.

He leaned forward and brushed the tears off her cheeks as they started to fall. "Maddie, I'm so sorry. It's my fault that you're here."

She turned her head more to look at him and winced

again. "Mark, what happened? Why am I here, and what's wrong with me?"

He watched her heartbeat quicken on the monitor. "It's okay. Calm down. You're safe and in the hospital. What do you remember from yesterday morning?"

She furrowed her brow as she thought about it. "I remember that I wanted to talk to you alone. Someone from your family was always around you, and I just wanted to apologize." She put her right hand on her head for a moment and then lowered it. "I remember being in the master closet and waiting for you, thinking that I was a creepy stalker."

He chuckled. Then he reached out and softly brushed her hair off her forehead.

"You arrived and were not happy about what I said." She scrunched up her face as she seemed to think about it. "Am I right, Mark? I remember trying to talk to you, but I don't remember what happened after that."

Okay. He could pretend he hadn't been a complete jerk, or he could be honest with her. It seemed like they needed to be honest with each other for a change instead of hiding their feelings. "I was angry, Maddie. I said mean things to you. It was the hurt inside me from years ago, and I did not give you a chance. I made you cry, and you ran out of the room."

"Did I fall then? My arm has scratches on it."

"No, you ran down the stairs, through the great room, and out the front door. You would have been okay, at least physically, but I didn't know anyone was in the house, so I'd set a toolbox on the step, knowing that I was going to come back outside shortly to use them. The best I can figure out is that you ran down the steps and tripped over it. I found you lying on the ground, unconscious." He closed his eyes and stopped talking for a moment. Then he opened them and stared into her eyes. "Maddie, that was the worst moment of my entire life. I thought I had lost you."

"You drove me to the hospital?"

"I called 9-1-1, and you were flown to Anchorage in a helicopter."

She gasped. The doctor walked in the door, doing his rounds. "I see my patient is doing much better than she was yesterday." He smiled broadly.

"Doctor, can you tell me what's wrong with me?"

Mark said, "I'll wait outside."

"No, Mark, you can stay unless they need to do some sort of examination that involves taking off my clothes."

Mark grinned. Maddie was back.

The doctor chuckled. "No, I think we've taken off all the clothes we're going to for right now. We were most concerned about your head and being unconscious for hours." He checked her eyes. "They focus well, so I think you're healing nicely. As to what happened—you broke your right ankle. From the abrasions on both arms, I think you covered your face with your arms to protect it. That may be why you broke your arm—right about here." He touched the middle of her left forearm. "You're going to be fine, though. We were concerned that it would be much worse when you first arrived. I'm sure that's why they sent you to us because a small hospital couldn't have helped you with those injuries."

"When can I leave?"

"With two broken limbs, it's going to be a little bit more challenging for you to get about, and you were unconscious for a long time. Those all add up to us keeping you here for a few days. Perhaps even longer."

To Mark, he said, "Take good care of your fiancée."

"Thank you, Doctor."

When he was gone, she said, "What was that about, Mark? I do have a memory of that not being true. Of you not wanting to have anything . . ." she choked up for a moment and cleared her throat, "to do with me."

"They wouldn't let me in the ambulance unless I was family, and that's the best I could come up with at the time. I wasn't going to let you out of my sight, Maddie. Please forgive me. It shouldn't have taken this to get me to realize how much you mean to me, how much you've always meant to me, but it did."

She watched him warily. "I don't know what to think. I'm confused. Maybe it's the drugs they've given me. I know I don't hurt anywhere, so that must mean I've been given some serious medication." She yawned and closed her eyes. Sounding half-awake, she added what sounded like, "I will always love you."

Maddie opened her eyes. An IV and medical technology around her reminded her of where she was. She'd been injured, and Mark had apologized. A vase with flowers in her favorite colors made a pretty statement at the side of her otherwise dreary room.

Jemma came in the door with her husband. Maddie smiled broadly at them. Mark tried to sneak out behind them without anyone noticing. Had he been here all this time?

Maddie called out to him, "Mark, has anyone contacted my sister or parents?"

He stopped. "I don't know, but I don't think so. We didn't

have your phone, so we didn't have the numbers."

"That's probably best. I'll call them soon. I think it's a lot better if they hear my voice on the phone now that I'm awake instead of someone telling them that I've had an accident, and I'm unconscious in the hospital."

Jemima answered, "That does sound much better."

Mark left.

Madeline greeted her friend, but before she could say anything more than "I'm glad to see you," Jemma interrupted her.

"It's my fault you're in this hospital bed. I'm sorry."

"Mark said it was his fault, and now you say it's your fault." Madeline rubbed her forehead. "I don't even know what to think."

"I wanted you and Mark to get together. He told us last night that he'd been mean to you when you apologized for everything that had happened when you were teenagers. And that he made you cry. Maddie, he tried to hide it, but he was crying when he told us."

Mark could cry? She hadn't thought that was possible. He seemed so buttoned up. Maybe there was hope for him after all.

"I know he's been very kind to me while I've been here. He told me what he'd done."

"I'm surprised at that. Do you want him in your life, Maddie? Are you done with him? We can help you either way."

CHAPTER SIXTEEN

*S*he had always loved him. She hadn't said those words out loud, had she? "Jemma, I think his anger yesterday was what he'd been storing up all those years. He told me how horrible it had been when he was in boot camp, and my email came. He'd been hurt and scared and all alone. I think it's time for some forgiveness all around. I'm not sure I have the answer for you right now. I think I need to get weaned off my medication just a little bit and think more clearly."

Her friend frowned at the IV bag hanging above her. "That makes sense. Is there anything you want or need?"

Maddie looked down at herself. "I'm wearing the world's ugliest nightgown. I don't know if I'm allowed to wear something better, but if they say I can, I would like that. And I think they're going to want me to walk once I'm in a cast, so a robe—also not ugly—would be a bonus. I don't know about footwear. What does one wear with one foot in a cast?"

Jemma grinned. "I think you're in better shape mentally than you realize. You sound like yourself." She stood. "I will

see what I can do on the not-ugly nightgown and robe front."
She wrote on a piece of paper and set it on the nightstand. "I
don't know where your phone is, but if you need me, this is
my number. Don't hesitate to call me anytime, and I'll get
you whatever you want."

"You're a good friend." Maddie felt her eyelids growing
heavy again.

"I just wish I hadn't gotten you into this mess in the first
place."

Maddie forced her eyelids open and looked up at her
friend. "Getting Mark and me back together may be the
greatest thing anyone's ever done for me."

The next thing she knew, she heard people talking in her
room. She opened her eyes to find Mrs. O'Connell, Andy,
and Mark standing around her bed.

Mrs. O'Connell said, "She's awake. Maddie, how are
you?"

How was she? Her head felt clearer. "I'm getting better,
thank you. I don't know how long I'm going to have to wear
these lovely fashion accessories, though." She lifted her left
arm a few inches and winced.

The older woman answered, "Probably six to eight weeks.
That's how it's been with everyone I know."

The pretty floral arrangement she'd noticed the last time
she was awake had multiplied to two. She wondered who
was sending them to her.

Mark stood hesitantly off to the side, but his mother and
Andy started for the door. His mother said, "We're going to
go down to the cafeteria to get a cup of coffee. We'll be back
soon, though."

When they were gone, Mark came over and sat next to

her. "I'm glad you're feeling better. I know everybody keeps asking you this, but is there anything you want?"

She pointed toward the floral arrangements. "Who are they from? Please go over there to see if there's an envelope in them."

He didn't move. "I brought them, Maddie."

She did not like it when people did things out of pity. "Mark, you didn't have to do that. You apologized and that's enough."

He held her hand again. "Maddie, those are partly to apologize, but really they're to court you." He looked into her eyes quite seriously when he said the word *court*.

She hadn't heard that word in, well, maybe her whole life outside of books, movies, or TV. Something about it caught her funny bone, and she giggled. "Mark, who told you to court me? That doesn't sound like you. Wait." She held up her hand. "Your mother? Or maybe a grandmother?"

He looked embarrassed when he said, "Mom. But I like the idea of showing you that I care about you. I am sorry. Can we please start over?"

"Mark, I feel like we started over when I found you underneath the sink in Jemma's house. We've been getting to know each other again. Right?"

He seemed to be pondering that, then surprise lit his face. "You're right. I felt close to you on many occasions. Did I undo everything when you apologized?"

"I barely remember what happened. I talked to the doctor this afternoon, and he said there's a good chance that I will never recover that moment of my memory. I remember talking to you and your expression. You did not look happy. That much, I know. As to the future, I'm not sure about that and a lot of things right now."

He looked crestfallen. "I understand. Do you mind if I visit you here every day?" He started to pull his hand away from hers, but she squeezed it and held on.

"I want you to be here. You *were* my best friend and more. It looks like I'm going to be lying here for a little while. But aren't you needed at the job site? I know your brothers have to go back to their own work soon. For their sakes, I don't want the job to take longer than it has to."

"Dad is taking over as the contractor when I'm not on site. I do need to go there now, though, if you don't mind. But I'll be back later tonight. Is that okay?"

She nodded, and he gave her a weak smile as he went out the door. He cared about her. A glimmer of hope that they could heal their relationship grew in her heart.

True to his word, Mark showed up every morning, then left for a while and returned in the evening. She knew that each trip took him about two hours round trip. That was a lot of driving, but the more time they spent together, the closer she felt to him. Now that they had talked about the past, the hurt and anger seemed to be sliding away. Maybe not completely and instantly, but she felt like she was seeing the Mark she had known before. He'd grown up too. He knew his mind and who he was. The boy she had known had been still forming and creating who he would become.

She was falling more deeply in love with this Mark. She hoped that he wasn't leading her up to a big fall.

Navigating the whole walking thing with one leg and arm immobilized had been more of a challenge than she'd expected, so they'd had physical therapy come to work with her multiple times every day. A few days at the hospital turned into a week.

Mark brought her a box of chocolates on the fourth day. He sat in the chair beside her hospital bed and opened the box. "I remembered that you love dark chocolate."

A delicious chocolate scent floated over. She plucked one out of the box. Popping it into her mouth, she closed her eyes. "Mmm. I feel happier already. But what are you going to eat?"

He chuckled. "I'm milk chocolate all the way, so these are for you."

She chose another piece. "Silly, misguided man. But I'll respect you anyway." She raised the back on her bed. "I need to walk. Do you want to go with me?"

He nervously looked over his shoulder toward the door. "Are you sure you should do that?"

Laughing, she swung her legs off the side of the bed. "This is doctor's orders. As appealing as it sounds, I don't get to lie in bed and eat chocolate all day."

He handed her the crutches and walked beside her as she hobbled out the room.

"How is my home's construction going?"

"Very well. You'll be pleased with all that's been done."

Being here meant that she couldn't follow her home's progress, and she missed that. "Can you take photos and show me?"

Silence greeted her.

She stopped and looked up at him. He seemed tense. "Is there a problem with my house?"

He rushed to say, "There aren't any problems. But I would like for there to be some surprises."

"I like surprises, but could I see photos of one room?"

Mark's shoulders relaxed. "Sure." He put his hand on her cheek and looked into her eyes. "I'll take photos of one room each day."

Joy raced through her, but not because of her house. If it didn't mean she might topple over and hit the floor, she would lean forward and kiss him. He seemed to feel the same, so he gave her a gentle kiss, then glanced around them as if he realized someone could be watching. He'd always been bold but shy at the same time.

The next day, he brought her an oddly-shaped package. When she took it from him, it felt soft under the wrapping paper. Peeling it away revealed a pillow in shades of blues and greens. "This is gorgeous! I'd love to have two of these on a sofa in the great room."

He leaned forward and kissed her. "I'm glad you love it that much because I did buy two of them."

Flowers and chocolates had been wonderful, but this meant he'd spent time choosing something uniquely her style.

"Jemma went to the store with me and helped choose it."

Madeline sighed. She had photos of designs she liked, but she wasn't sure she could pull it off. "Yes. I'd like to have her decorate my entire house, but I don't think she's in my budget. She offered to do it for free, but I don't want to take advantage of a friend."

He shrugged. "Think about it." Mark pulled his phone out of his pocket. "Today's photos are of your master bath." He held up his phone so she could see each photo.

"It's more beautiful than I imagined and so fast." She didn't know how they'd pulled it off. "I can't wait to see it in person."

When it was *finally* the day for her to be released, Jemma offered to take her home, and she agreed. But when the time came for her friend to arrive, Mark walked in the door. "Mark, I am so sorry, but Jemma offered to take me home, and I felt like I needed to say yes to her. She's been so good to me."

"Don't worry. I heard through the family grapevine that she was bringing you home. I called her and asked if I could do it instead. I rented a sedan so it would be easier for you to climb into than my truck."

Her old Mark had been sweet, but this new version of him had treated her so kindly. "I could have done it." At his expression of disbelief, she tried to picture herself stepping up into his truck with her healthy leg and pulling the broken foot in behind her, using the injured arm for support. "Maybe not."

He chuckled.

When an orderly arrived with the compulsory wheelchair for her hospital departure, Mark left to move the car nearer the door. He was waiting downstairs with a large sedan as he had promised. As they drove, they talked about things from their childhood and things to do with the house.

"I'd love to see what my house looks like after a week. But I don't know if I can walk on the uneven ground with a walking cast. And I definitely haven't tried stairs yet."

He turned onto the road that led to her house. "I've had the driveway graded and the gravel put down. I think you'll be able to walk, but if not, I'll carry you in."

She was about to argue that, then realized being carried in Mark's arms didn't sound like a bad thing. Sitting back in her seat, she grinned. She was starting to think that maybe, just maybe, the two of them could have a life together.

At her house, he helped her out of the car, but slogging through the gravel was difficult, so he swept her up in his arms and held her to his chest as he strode purposefully to the stairs and into the house. Inside, he brought her over to a blanket on the floor in the center of her great room and gently set her on it. A roaring fire in the stone fireplace warmed the room, maybe too much in July, but she still loved it.

As she relaxed in *her* home, she looked around and realized that the room had furniture and accessories, ones she loved.

It was complete.

"Mark?" She couldn't get the words out. She gestured around the room. Then she leaned to the side to see into the kitchen. She could see enough of it to know that the cabinets and the counters, the tile she had chosen, it all seemed to be done. There was even a bowl of fruit on the island. She looked up at him. "How did you do this?"

He grinned. "We wanted to surprise you. We were a little concerned that they'd let you out even faster. We put the finishing touches on it this morning. Everyone in my family helped. Jemma did the decorating with the help of my mother. You'll notice a few inevitable bits of floral scattered throughout the house."

She grinned. "That's okay with me. I do admire Jemma's decorating style, though. Is the upstairs done too? Do I have a master bedroom?"

"You do. But you can't manage the stairs yet, Maddie. We finished the downstairs office as your bedroom for now.

That way, you'll have access to a bathroom, the kitchen, and all of the main living space."

The doors to the office room were closed, and there was something on the glass so she couldn't see through it. "Is there something wrong with the doors?"

"Well, if you're using it as a bedroom, we thought you'd want some privacy. Once your life is back to normal, you can just take the paper down. That's all it is."

"That makes sense." He opened the doors so that she could see inside. "It's very pretty. Thank you. For everything."

She realized that he'd set a scene when he went into the kitchen and returned with a picnic basket.

"You wanted to have a picnic in front of a roaring fire." Mark put the basket on the blanket. He made plates for each of them with fried chicken legs, coleslaw, and fruit salad.

He handed one to her and she greedily dug into it. "I'm very hungry." She bit into the chicken. "Wonderful!"

He grinned sheepishly. "I'm glad you're enjoying it. I wanted good food, so I asked Nathaniel to make it for me."

"Not your mother?" The fruit salad was a vibrant combination of summer fruits. "This is delicious too."

He laughed. "I think you're just tired of hospital food."

"Not that he isn't a great cook, but that's entirely possible." As Madeline devoured her food, she realized that Mark had eaten a similar amount. That wasn't his norm.

"To answer your question, Mom and Dad are exploring the area around Chicken."

"That's a fun area to check out." When she'd finished what he'd served her, she still had room for more, "I'm being greedy, but is there dessert?"

Mark gulped. "Cupcakes." He smiled. Sort of.

He'd gone from confident to nervous. Why? "Who made the cupcakes?"

He set one on a plate. "I bought them at a bakery. My culinary skills don't extend to baking."

"So you love my baking skills?"

His breath hitched, and he fidgeted nervously. Turning toward her, he held the cupcake where she could see it. An engagement ring more than twice the normal size rested on top of white frosting.

"Mark?"

When he knelt in front of her, her heart began racing. "I love *you*, Maddie McGuire. I know this seems sudden, but it's something that we should have done a long time ago. I have always and only loved you. Will you do me the honor of becoming my wife?" He waited silently.

"Yes! Of course, I'll marry you. I love you!"

He gently pulled her close and kissed her. Leaning his forehead against hers, he said, "I almost bought you a ring, but I thought you'd like to choose it yourself."

"It will be fun choosing our rings *together*." She leaned forward to kiss him, wishing she could wrap both arms around him. When she leaned too far, the weight of her cast started to pull her down, but he caught her.

"Was it your injuries or the power of our kiss that made you wobbly?" He grinned at her.

"You should kiss me again so I can check."

He did as his fiancée asked.

BONUS EPILOGUE

"*A*ny update on your matchmaking attempt, Jemma?" Bree asked as her sisters Jemma and Holly entered her condo, Holly with a pie in her hands.

Holly grinned. "Adam told me that Mark proposed to Madeline yesterday! I didn't think the match would work, but Jemma knew that Mark and Madeline belonged together."

Bree raised her baby's hand in salute.

Holly turned to Bree. "Jemma's their official matchmaker. That's one for me with Noah and Rachel, one for Jemma, and . . ."

Bree smiled as she played with her baby. "I'm finally ready to help. Even as a pediatrician, I've been surprised by a new mother's lack of sleep. Now that Petey is sleeping through the night, I'm ready to be the matchmaker."

Holly asked, "Any ideas for Jack or Andy? You haven't been out and about much lately."

"That's okay. I know the perfect woman for Jack."

Jemma pursed her lips. "I'd thought Andy would be next.

He's always smiling, so he seems like an easy one to match up."

Bree frowned. "I don't have anyone for him. Do either of you?"

"Not me," Holly said.

Jemma added, "I haven't come up with anyone for Andy either, but Jack may be a little tougher to match. I think he's quite happy with his new life."

Her sisters were right. But still . . .

"Who do you have in mind for him?"

"Mark was with Madeline at the hospital when I stopped by to visit her a couple of days ago. When he left to get a cup of coffee, I followed him out and asked about where he planned to buy her engagement ring."

Jemma gasped. "You didn't!"

Bree nodded. "I did. Everyone could see what was happening with them. And I had a plan for Jack that tied into them."

Holly motioned forward with her hand. "Tell us what happened when you asked."

"He blushed bright red and glanced around, as though he didn't want anyone to overhear. He said that he'd been too busy at the hospital to shop, so he'd decided to shop for the rings with Maddie when she's better."

Petey made happy sounds, and she smiled at him. "I must say that I was relieved. I have the perfect plan." But would they agree?

Jemma stared at her sister. "You aren't making sense. A ring for one brother's fiancée and matchmaking for a different brother don't connect." Jemma and Holly glanced at each other and nodded. "We both understand if new mother-hood has overwhelmed you."

Both Holly and Jemma wore concerned expressions.

Bree smiled smugly. "Mark needs a ring. I know a fabulous jeweler. It's perfect."

"Why perfect?" Jemma held up her hands in frustration. "You're the logical one, but you aren't making sense. We're still talking about matchmaking, aren't we?"

"We are. Jack is a jeweler. The woman I have in mind for Jack owns a jewelry store."

Jemma held her head. "You're confusing me." She pulled her hands away. "Hold it! Do you want to send Jack in to buy rings for Mark and Madeline?"

She gave a single nod, then picked Petey up and cradled him next to her. "Yes. She sells rings, and they need rings." This would be her first matchmaking attempt, and she knew she'd chosen well.

Jemma sighed. "Bree, this is the same Jack O'Connell who invited everyone to a party the day he *sold his jewelry store.* He's now pursuing his dream of being a nature and landscape photographer."

For the first time, Bree's excitement dimmed. "Well, yes. But I know they'd be great together." She sat defiantly, and Petey looked up at her. "We supported your idea that Mark and Madeline should get back together. That one was touch and go for a while."

Jemma shrugged. "True. You've been quiet, Holly. What do you think?"

Holly got up and went into the kitchen, talking to them over the kitchen island as she fixed a cup of coffee. "Since I haven't met this woman—what's her name?"

"Aimee."

"I haven't met Aimee, so I don't know if this will work." Holly held up a mug. "Anyone else want tea or coffee with their pie?" She raised one eyebrow. "I assume you both want a slice of lemon meringue pie."

"Of course." Jemma joined Holly in the kitchen and gathered the plates and forks they'd need. "How do you propose we get them together, Bree?"

Bree stood and went over to the island. "I have what I hope is a great plan. Even I know it's a bit of a reach, though."

Holly expertly slid a piece of pie onto a plate. "And if it doesn't?"

What would she do? "I'll try again with them. They deserve more than one chance to be a couple. I know I have this right."

Jemma and Holly glanced at each other and shrugged. "If you're sure they'll be happy together—"

Bree grinned. "We're sure, aren't we, Petey?" Apparently bored with the women, her baby's eyes closed.

Jemma laughed. "I don't think he cares."

"Jack and Aimee are perfect for each other." She hesitated for a second. "But there may be some bumpy roads along the way."

Jemma's eyebrows shot up. "I'm curious about this one." She held up her mug. "Here's to the *first* attempt at their match."

WHAT'S NEXT?

Mark's brother Jack is the next O'Connell to meet his match. This match is more challenging because a jewelry store is the last place Jack wants to be and Aimee owns one. Have the matchmakers made a mistake this time? Or is there hope for Jack and Aimee in *Hopefully Matched?*

WHAT'S AFTER THAT?

Each of the O'Connell brothers meet their match in the Alaska Matchmakers Romance series. But matchmakers Jemma, Bree, and Holly met their husbands in the Alaska Dream Romance series. If you haven't read them yet, you don't want to miss *Falling for Alaska* (Jemma's story), *Loving Alaska* (Bree's story), and *Crazy About Alaska*, (Holly and Adam's story).

Also,

There's a FREE, short story tied to these books. Pete and Cathy are in *Falling for Alaska*. Pete—Nathaniel's lawyer— and Cathy—a woman on a hike with Jemma—are minor characters, but their cute first meeting is a FREE short story. I liked them so much that I brought them back in *Crazy About Alaska*. Get your FREE short story by going to cathrynbrown.com/together.

ABOUT CATHRYN

Writing books that are fun and touch your heart

Even though Cathryn Brown always loved to read, she didn't plan to be a writer. She earned two degrees from the University of Alaska, one in journalism/public communications, but didn't become a journalist.

Years passed. Cathryn felt pulled into a writing life, testing her wings with a novel and moving on to articles. She's now an award-winning journalist who has sold hundreds articles to local, national, and regional publications.

The Feather Chase, written as Shannon L. Brown, was her first published book and begins the Crime-Solving Cousins Mystery series. The eight-to-twelve-year-olds in your life will enjoy this contemporary twist on a Nancy Drew–type mystery.

Cathryn enjoys hiking, sometimes while dictating a book. She also unwinds by baking and reading.

Cathryn lives in Nashville, Tennessee, with her professor husband and adorable calico cat.

Made in United States
Orlando, FL
22 November 2021

10624314R00121